DADAFARIN

or, The Pessimism

Allen Grove

Aliengrove Multimedia

The characters and events portrayed in this book are fictitious. Any similarity to real persons, living or dead, is coincidental and not intended by the author.

ISBN-13: 978-1-7399884-1-8

Cover design by: Aliengrove Multimedia
Printed in United Kingdom

To J

CONTENTS

"How changed Zarathustra is! Zarathustra has become a child, an awakened one. What do you plan to do in the land of the sleepers? You have been floating in a sea of solitude, and the sea has borne you up. At long last, are you ready for dry land? Are you ready to drag yourself ashore?"

Friedrich Nietzsche, Thus Spake Zarathustra

PROLOGUE

On a rare sunny day, on a beach in the county of Kent on the south coast of the country once known as Great Britain, a group of young men, eighteen in number, celebrate their arrival in a new land with cheers and raised fists. Some take selfies with their phones, several kiss the pebbles on the beach, while others gather their meagre belongings from a dinghy, now empty, bobbing gently in the surf. A few wave to a departing coastguard boat which had accompanied them for the last few miles of their journey. With a blast from it's horn, the boat sets off to escort more people making the perilous journey across one of the world's busiest shipping lanes, stopping briefly to pick up another, smaller dinghy that has been washed out to sea. Three of the men separate from the main group, breaking into a run, heading further along the beach, disappearing behind some sand dunes. After discarding their life jackets, the rest start walking across the beach towards a road, where several police men and women are apparently waiting for them. None of the police chase after the three men who have run off, though two policemen walk slowly towards the group of men making their way across the pebbled beach.

For these officers of the law this has become a daily ritual, greeting refugees from lands far and wide, people fleeing persecution, war, poverty or the law. Originating from countries as far away as Syria, Morocco, Vietnam and Sudan, lured by a glorious vision of England and Britain gained from music, radio, television and films, these refugees have undergone months or even years of privation, enduring heat, cold, hunger and more than a little resentment from the peoples of the countries they have passed through. They are among the most determined of the thousands entering Europe from Asia and Africa. They have never been deterred from their dreams of the promised land, travelling across the entire continent to that most famous of the European democracies, Great Britain.

Diverse in culture and religion, the one thing these latest new arrivals have in common is that they are all young men in their twenties, gripped with a grand vision of succeeding in a country famed throughout the world as the most free and fair of them all. They have come in search of a better life, a life where they would no longer have to worry about where the next meal comes from, and nice girls don't necessarily expect you to marry them if you want sex. Many have heard that you don't even need to work to get money. Britain, they have heard, is so welcoming to refugees that the government puts you up in an hotel when you arrive.

It is among these brave and adventurous men, walking slightly apart from the main group, that we first find our hero.

Walking slightly apart from the others is a young man of around twenty-five years of age, hands in pockets, hunched against the cold breeze's chill as he walks away from the calm steely grey sea. Of swarthy complexion and medium height and build, he looks fit and healthy. He has dark straight hair that reached to his shoulders, and is quite attractive in appearance, his light brown eyes radiating a glint of humour, or good faith. His name is Dadafarin, and his first steps in this new land have filled him brim full of excitement and anticipation. Escaping a troubled past, he looks forward to a new life: a life full of hope, freedom, and fairness. He can barely suppress his excitement. Life was going to get better, he knew it.

On the beach-front road a police van, which has evidently been waiting for them, disgorges several more uniformed officers, who then stand waiting by their vehicles, arms crossed, as the men approach. The new arrivals all look to have been expecting this, as none show surprise as they are asked questions, given survival blankets to keep warm, and handed small bottles of water and surgical masks, which they are instructed to put on immediately. A policeman asks the young man's name.

'Dadafarin' he answers. 'Dadafarin Engineer.'

'Engineer?' the policeman says, smiling sardonically. 'Doesn't sound very foreign to me.' He asks Dadafarin to spell his name, writing it in a notepad. 'And where are you from?' the policeman enquires.
'I am from Iran. I want to live in England.'
'You and half the world' the policeman replies, winking at one of his colleagues. 'Passport?'
'I have no passport' Dadafarin replies. The policeman does not seem in the least bit surprised at this. He writes in his notepad again, then moves to the next man. And so the adventure begins.

I
DADAFARIN FINDS HIMSELF IN PARADISE

Dadafarin stood apart from the other refugees, gazing across the English Channel. Having always been fascinated by history, he knew that this stretch of water had once been considered Britain's moat. In the distance, he could see another dinghy being intercepted by the coastguard, and wondered to himself how many more were still to come. Having foiled Spanish armadas and the Nazi navy, who would have thought that people in rubber boats would be the first large group of foreigners to land uninvited on these shores since the Battle of Fishguard in 1797?

Dadafarin was startled from his reverie by someone shouting at him. It was time to go. The assembled men were herded into two large vans with uncomfortable seats, assured by one of the policemen that it was not going to be a long journey as he shut the door. Dadafarin said nothing on the journey, in spite of some of the other men trying to engage him in conversation in several different languages. Dadafarin was a man who only spoke when he thought it necessary; he was often considered shy and reserved, a trait that had served him well in the past. Many of the men were busy texting their friends back in Calais, keeping them updated on their progress. Several of them discussed where they were being sent; one claimed he had overheard that they were being taken straight to an hotel, due to the processing facility near Dover being full. Dadafarin dozed, waking with a start as he was jolted by the police van turning off the road. Craning his neck, Dadafarin peered through the small reinforced glass window into the cab of the van.

Situated at the end of a long sweeping driveway through deciduous woodland appeared what looked like a stately home; it had in fact once been the home of a minor member of the aristocracy, whose current descendant now suffered the consequences of his ancestor's interests in a sugar plantation in Barbados nearly three hundred years earlier. A sign showed it had been renamed The Georgian Hotel, and had four
stars.

Disembarking the vans, the men were led through an elaborate portico into an open and spacious reception area, evidently recently modernised. At a long wooden counter, two men in uniform waited. A young girl in a uniform several sizes too small offered them welcome drinks of fruit juice. Then they were asked to register. Dadafarin had no trouble filling out the form, though several of the other young men appeared to be struggling. Dadafarin helped two of the other young refugees to fill in their registration forms. As they gave Dadafarin the information he needed, he found out that one was named

Noureldine, and hailed from Syria. The other was Ali, a huge bearded man from Turkey. Although he spoke good English, Noureldine said he had trouble writing the wrong way round, from left to right. Noureldine somehow unsettled Dadafarin, a scar across his acned face coupled with a perpetual scowl indicating that this man might have a rather suspect history. After registering, they were all given key-cards, and escorted to their rooms. The young man who showed Dadafarin to his room told him that dinner was served at 6pm.

The room was beautiful. Never in his wildest imagination had Dadafarin imagined himself to one day be resident in such a fine establishment. The bed was huge, the room was panelled with dark wood, and the bathroom was large enough to accommodate an entire extended family. A large bay window looked out from the third floor of the hotel onto a large green expanse of lawn, bordered by flower beds iridescent with flowering plants. Beyond the lawns, a dense forest hid the property from the main road. After several minutes admiring the view and looking through the drawers in the desk, which contained writing paper and a brochure on the local attractions, Dadafarin took a shower and put on the only other items of clothing he had brought with him, a fresh pair of pants and socks. Putting on his dirty shirt, jeans and black hoodie, he took a last look at the room, drinking in it's splendour, before heading down to dinner.

Dinner was a buffet consisting of chicken

soup, a selection of salads, and the choice of chicken curry or something called tofu, which looked like paneer. A small card declared this substance to be Vegan, which reminded Dadafarin of one his favourite TV shows, Star Trek, and resulted in him putting some on his plate. Dadafarin sat alone, several of the other refugees eyeing him occasionally while he was eating.

Dadafarin discovered that tofu had very little texture, and no taste whatsoever. The curry was pleasant, but not very spicy. Most of the men ate with their fingers though Ali, the huge bearded Kurd from Turkey, stabbed his food viciously with a fork before putting it in his mouth. Noureldine, the Syrian, evidently disapproved of the menu, pulling faces as he stuffed food in his mouth. After chewing his food with evident distaste, Noureldine gesticulated at his plate while cursing quietly in Arabic. Dadafarin used the knife and fork, enjoying the unfamiliar food, though he decided that tofu was not something he was going to seek out in the future. He ate quietly, while the other men talked continually, in many different languages.

Dadafarin could sense that many of these men seemed distrustful of him, perhaps due his apparent lack of sociability. He had no desire for conversation anyway, and was looking forward to getting back to the luxury of his new accommodation. After finishing his meal with a slice of lemon cake, he went back to his room, threw himself onto the soft bed and flicked through the television channels. On the BBC, much to his surprise, two people were arguing about whether the police in Britain were racist. After a few minutes, he switched off the television, and wandered into the bathroom. The hotel had provided soap, towels, and even a toothbrush and toothpaste. After enjoying the luxury of a second shower and brushing his teeth, he climbed into the bed, which to his delight felt very comfortable. By ten o'clock, he was fast asleep.

II
DADAFARIN MEETS DR VENNGLOSS AND CAREY

The next morning Dadafarin woke early and went to breakfast at 8am. A selection of cereals, bread, cheese, fruit and hard-boiled eggs was laid out on two tables against one wall. The buffet also featured bacon alongside a tray of fried eggs, much to the disgust of most of the guests. Noureldine complained loudly in English to one of the waiters about the lack of halal food, and received assurances from the restaurant manager that never again would they be insulted by seeing pork or any other haram food on the menu. This seemed to satisfy most of the guests, and they tucked into fried eggs, toast, butter and jam. Ali, however, did not look so happy, but tried hard not to show it. He had accidentally eaten several slices of bacon before the others pointed out to him that it was pork. He then accidentally ate another two slices before he reacted with surprised indignation. He caught Dadafarin's gaze as he rolled his eyes, and so they shared a common secret. They both liked bacon.

After breakfast the new arrivals were asked to go into a conference room, where a number of people in masks were waiting. As they entered, a thermometer device was pointed at their foreheads before they were ushered towards two rows of seats at the back of the room, all the chairs spaced two metres apart. A row of four desks, each with two people sitting behind them, were placed in line across the other end of the room. They were invited to sit until their names were called. A young man in a huge pullover informed them that interpreters were available, should they need them. Dadafarin did not need an interpreter, and he doubted that any of the officials would speak Farsi anyway. Dadafarin spoke very good English, though with a strong accent. His name was one of the first called, and he made his way to the desk indicated and sat down opposite a young man at a desk. This young man looked very strange, with long brown hair and a piece of metal shaped like a bone stuck through his septum, and a single earring in his left ear lobe.

An older woman sat about a metre off to the side. She was dressed in what looked like men's clothes, including a tweed jacket. She had short curly hair with a slight blue tint to it, and wore a pair of horn-rimmed glasses, reminding Dadafarin of a character he had once seen on an old black and white television show. Neither introduced themselves. The lady first asked him his name, his date of birth, and where he had entered Europe.

'I am Dadafarin Engineer, from Iran' Dadafarin replied. 'I was born on the 1st of May, 1995. I have travelled from Turkey and then Greece. It has taken me many months.'

'Did you register in any European country when

you first arrived, or since?' she asked.
'No. I was never asked to' he replied.
The young man then asked him why he was fleeing his country.
'Religious persecution.'
'And what is your religion?' the young man asked.
'Mazdayasna.' The man and woman looked at each other, evidently confused. 'Most people call us Zoroastrians' Dadafarin explained.
'Wow, is that a thing?' the man asked. 'I thought it was invented by Nietzsche.'
'It is one of the world's oldest religions.' Dadafarin informed him. 'It is the one true faith.' He finished the sentence with a smile, so as not embarrass the young man further.
'And what is your occupation?' the pierced man continued.
'I am a mechanic. A motorcycle mechanic. I did start a degree in history, but the university removed me.'
'Removed you? What for?'
'I did not declare my religion when I applied. The government in Iran does not like people who are not Muslim. Ba'hai people have been expelled from university for their religion, and I thought it best to leave the space on the form blank. I thought they would not want a Zoroastrian studying history. The history of Mazdayasna in Iran is not very flattering to their cause.'

The question that most surprised Dadafarin was when the young man asked him his gender.

'What do you mean?' he asked.
'Your gender. Do you identify as male, female, non-binary? Genderfluid? Or something else? What pronouns do you use?'
'Pronouns? What do pronouns have to do with my gender? I am a man.'

At this point, the woman cut in. 'Sorry, Mr Engineer. Some people are not comfortable with their birth gender, as it does not reflect who they actually are. Shall we put down that you are a cis-gender male?'
They agreed upon this, although Dadafarin had no idea what cisgender meant. It sounded vaguely derogatory, he thought. The woman looked a bit disappointed. At that, the interview was concluded, and Dadafarin was asked to go into a conference room where the men all collected after their brief interviews, sitting on chairs arranged in lines in front of a whiteboard.

After they had all finished registering for asylum, they were given a presentation on the current Covid rules by an older man in a suit. Next to him stood a very pretty nurse who they were told was from the local clinic,. The clinic would be dealing with any ailments they had while staying in the hotel. The country was currently in full lockdown, the man announced, although this was likely to end soon. However, local lockdowns would probably still be enforced periodically, and the hotel would put up a notice board announcing the current restrictions. They weren't allowed to leave the hotel grounds without good reason, and couldn't visit each others rooms. They should avoid socialising, and maintain a distance of two metres between themselves and anyone else. Masks, although not yet mandatory, soon would be; they were encouraged to wear them at all times in public areas. Sanitiser stations were dotted around the hotel, and they were expected, in the interests of public safety, to make full use of them.

The nurse then demonstrated how to wash your hands, and how to apply sanitiser. The whole presentation was done in English, with two translators standing to either side repeating the instructions in Arabic and Urdu. The Prime Minister had recently had the disease, they were told, so no-one was immune. Vigilance was needed.

After the presentation, they were invited to go into another conference room, where a small group of people were gathered, all wearing masks. In spite of the masks, their body language and eyes indicated they were very happy to meet the refugees. A large banner proclaimed WELCOME TO OUR REFUGEES, FROM THE BENEVOLENT CHURCH OF JESUS CHRIST THE REDEEMER. Noureldine didn't look too happy, but a few quiet words from his companions had him smiling, and apparently now very happy to see them.

Laid out on several tables were clothes, some books, and bags containing toiletries. The men were invited to find any clothes that fit and help themselves to the books and toiletries. Ini-

tially there was a rush to the tables, but a loud male voice shouted at them not to push in, there was plenty for everyone. They formed two lines and made their way along the line of tables. Dadafarin found some trousers, a buttoned shirt, and a slightly tatty black down jacket, similar to the one Noureldine wore. He'd hoped to find some new trainers, but none fitted him. A couple approached him as he left the table full of gifts. One was a thin balding man who appeared to be in his early fifties, wearing jeans, a T shirt and a jacket that looked like it was part of a cheap suit. The other, a young girl with pale blonde hair, wore jeans and a tight yellow T shirt which accentuated her pert bosom. The couple invited him out onto the terrace, where they removed their masks.
'Ah, that's better' said the girl, smiling at Dadafarin. He couldn't believe his eyes. She was exceptionally beautiful. She was quite short, with straight blonde hair, vibrant green eyes, and a cute freckled nose, slightly upturned at the tip. Dadafarin tried not to stare.

The man introduced himself first, but did not offer his hand. 'I'm Dr Anton Venngloss. We are both from Justice In Exile, and we help refugees settle here. We are a registered charity, funded by donors worldwide. I have been assigned to your case.' Dr Venngloss smiled, handing Dadafarin an embossed business card. After admiring the business card briefly, Dadafarin put it in his pocket.

Quite who had assigned Dr Venngloss to

him, Dadafarin never discovered, as it appeared from his business card that the doctor was, in fact, the chairperson of the charity. However, it marked the start of a great friendship.
'And I am Carey' The young woman added. 'I am a part-time volunteer. We are so glad to have you here.'
'I am Dadafarin. My friends call me Dada. What makes you so glad to have me here?'
Carey seemed a bit taken aback by this.'Well, it must have been terrible. The journey. The trauma in your homeland?'
'Yes, they don't like us in Iran. Much persecution.' Dadafarin was trying very hard not to stare at her.
'Well, you're safe now' Dr Venngloss interrupted. 'Here we believe in a world where everyone is equal. Especially if they are from a group that has traditionally suffered persecution. You'll find things are very different here to your homeland.'
'I have been heavily persecuted' Dadafarin reiterated, looking down at Dr Venngloss' bright red shoes.
'Well, you're safe now' Dr Venngloss repeated. 'I will give you my 'phone number, and you must call me any time you want.'

Dadafarin was hoping the young girl would offer her number too, but she just smiled, her beautiful green eyes radiating warmth and empathy.
'I have lost my 'phone.' Dadafarin replied. 'I don't have money for a new one'

'Don't worry' Carey reassured him. 'We always carry a few spare 'phones.' She looked in her handbag, then pulled out a brand-new 'phone, the screen still with a plastic film attached. 'Both of our numbers are in the address book, along with Lesley's. You'll meet Lesley soon. They are dealing with the legal side of your case. Our job is to make sure you are comfortable, and to ensure your asylum claim goes smoothly.'

'The phone has got £30 of credit on it' Dr Venngloss added. He then pulled a wallet out of his pocket and pulled out a crisp large note. 'Here is twenty pounds in cash too, which you can repay when your benefits are paid. I have to talk to the others, and we have another hotel to visit. But I will be back tomorrow, and we can get to know one another better.'

With that, Dr Venngloss and Carey wandered off to talk to the other refugees, leaving Dadafarin admiring the view across the lawns and flower beds of the beautifully manicured gardens. The sun beat down from an azure sky, and he could hear birds tweeting from the line of trees edging the lawn. Dadafarin decided he liked this new life. He loved the idea of everyone being truly equal, or perhaps even better.

On the way back to his room, he asked the receptionist if he could take the newspaper he had seen on a table in the foyer.

'Yes, take it. We get papers delivered every day.' she replied. 'No-one ever cancelled the deliveries when we closed to the public.'

Dadafarin picked up the newspaper, which was called The Sentinel. On the front page, there was a picture of a crowd of people throwing a statue into a harbour in a place called Bristol, next to an article accusing the government of ignorance on racism in the United Kingdom. Having also seen a discussion on racism the night before on the BBC, this came as a real shock to Dadafarin. Of all the things he had expected to find in Britain, racism was not one of them. He hoped that the British would not hate him just because he was foreign. Tucking the paper under his arm, he helped himself to a cup of coffee from the free coffee machine near the elevators, then pressed the button to call the lift. He looked forward to reading the articles. It seemed something was going on in Britain. He decided to find out more.

III
DR VENNGLOSS EXPLAINS RACISM

The next day, Dr Vennglоss arrived at the hotel just after 9am. Dadafarin was still in bed when the receptionist called to say that Dr Vennglоss was waiting downstairs in the lobby for him. Dadafarin quickly washed his face, brushed his teeth, and got dressed. He realised he had missed breakfast, and felt a bit hungry. He had slept a bit later than intended. Next time he would set an alarm. He'd stayed up late, lost in thought after reading about the demonstration in Bristol. He'd watched the ten o'clock news on the BBC, which, overall, seemed in favour of the day's events. After pulling down the statue of Edward Colston, a slave trader from the 17th Century who had used the money he made to build most of Bristol, the demonstrators had been praised by the media.

The Sentinel talked of the evils of slavery and the institutionalised worship of imperialist idols, and the mayor of Bristol himself welcomed the modifications made to his city by graffiti artists, pyromaniacs and vandals. Police had knelt on one knee and watched happily as the crowd pulled the statue from it's plinth and threw it into the harbour. Evidently destroying statues of long-dead people somehow also gave you an exemption from the Covid restrictions, as nowhere in the article did it mention the pandemic. Further into the paper, Dadafarin read an article about Scotland wanting independence.

The leader of Scotland, Giselle Trout, wanted a second referendum, as apparently the previous one, where the Scottish people had rejected independence, was invalid, due to the government in London deceiving the voters. The United Kingdom was apparently not as united as its name suggested.

Dadafarin had also used his new phone to look up Dr Venngloss on the free hotel internet. It turned out that Dr Anton Venngloss was quite famous. He had obtained a PhD in sociology from the University of Kent. He had then taken up a teaching post at the University of Bradford, where he had received critical acclaim for a paper he had written titled 'De-constructing heteronormative orthodoxy in animal husbandry: the role of neuro-linguistic patriarchy in agriculture.' Reviewers had apparently especially liked the title of this paper, which succinctly summed up the paper in one bold statement. A few critics had apparently claimed the irony in the use of the word “husbandry” was unintentional, and that Dr Venngloss was just spouting nonsense, but these were a quickly silenced minority.

After ten years in Bradford, Dr Venngloss had returned to Kent and founded the charity Justice in Exile, which was dedicated to assisting migrants fleeing war and persecution. Although Dadafarin didn't understand quite what Dr Vennglosss's paper was about, it was apparent that Dr Vennglosss was truly a man committed to fairness in all walks of life. Dadafarin very much liked Dr Vennglosss's business card, which was embossed with the logo of Justice in Exile, consisting of an old-style balance scale superimposed on a globe, with large embossed letters, a J and an E, placed in the pans on either side of the scale. On the reverse of the card were Dr Vennglosss' Twitter and Instagram names. Dadafarin had heard of Twitter, though had never actually seen it before. He decided to set up a new account, using his recently acquired phone, and Dr Vennglosss became the first person he was following.

A lot of Dr Vennglosss' posts consisted of what Dadafarin discovered were "retweets", where Dr Vennglosss had shared posts he evidently approved of. All of them appeared to be related to social justice or critical of the government. Dadafarin quickly worked out how to follow these retweeted people too, and very soon his Twitter feed started filling up with new tweets. Dadafarin decided he would explore Twitter further over the coming days.

After checking himself in the mirror, Dadafarin made his way downstairs. Dr Vennglosss greeted him warmly, though declined to shake hands, instead proffering an elbow. Unsure what was expected of him, Dadafarin shook the doctor's elbow, eliciting a smile.

'We bump elbows now, with Covid.' Dr Venngloss then demonstrated how to do an elbow bump. The doctor appeared to be wearing the same clothes as the day before. He handed Dadafarin an envelope. 'This is your debit card. It should have your first weeks payment on it already.'

Dadafarin opened the envelope with a feeling of excitement. Inside was a blue plastic bank card, his name in raised type on the front below the account number.

'Thank you, Doctor' he said. 'Now I feel like I am a real person again.'

They took a walk in the hotel grounds, which looked even more beautiful than Dadafarin remembered. Stands of flowering larkspur, giant daisies and allium in well-manicured flower beds were dotted around the lawns. A scent of lavender greeted them as they turned towards the woods. An old man in a floppy hat was tending to some flowers in a bed, and greeted them warmly as they passed. After a few comments on the weather, and questions on how Dadafarin was settling in, Dr Venngloss asked Dadafarin about his life in Iran. Dadafarin explained how he had come to flee the terror of the Ayatollahs, who had no place in their Islamic republic for minorities such as Zoroastrians.

'I came to realise that if I wanted to achieve anything in my life, I would have to leave Iran' Dadafarin explained. 'My family were originally shipbuilders and civil engineers. It is how we came to have the name Engineer. That is what my ancestors were. Many fled to India, but my family stayed. My grandfather Ramin was the last in my family to actually be an engineer. In Iran now, we are lucky to find jobs cleaning the streets.'

'That is really shocking' Dr Venngloss said. 'Here in Britain you should be able to follow the path of your forebears, if you so choose. We do not tolerate discrimination. Everyone must be equal under the law.'

Dadafarin was very happy to hear this. He told Dr Venngloss of his dream of manufacturing custom motorcycles, and of his joy in renovating an old BSA motorcycle which his father had bought after the war and then left in a shed for many years. Dadafarin had even fabricated a few parts for it himself, he announced proudly.

As they followed a path through the woods, Dr Venngloss asked a question that at first caused some confusion.

'What are your opinions on race, Dada?'

'You mean like MotoGP?' Dadafarin asked. 'I like it very much. I very much admire Valentino Rossi. I watch all the races I can. I often dream of working for a team in MotoGP.'

'No, sorry, I am not talking about motor sport. I mean people's ethnicity. The group to which they belong.'

'Everyone belongs to something' Dadafarin replied.

'Yes, of course. But the differences between them

often cause problems. Historically, one group always becomes dominant and persecutes the rest. Like you Zoroastrians in Iran. I read something of your people's history on Wikipedia last night.' Dr Vennglоss looked at Dadafarin as if expecting approval.

Dadafarin gave him a grin. 'Yes, we are persecuted. Damn Muslims, horrible people!'

'No, no, they are not horrible. You can't judge a whole religion because of a few zealots. I have many Muslim friends. The problem is systemic racism and patriarchy, it's not religion.'

'Systemic racism?'

'Yes. Iran is controlled by supremacists who have established a religious elite. Here and in America, it is the capitalists, the white people. They have been building society in their own image for thousands of years. The very structure of society itself is racist. Everything here in the West is stacked against minorities, especially black and transgendered people.'

'But aren't you a white person?'

'Yes, and I am ashamed of it. I was born into privilege. In spite of being born to a father who was a coal miner, and a mother who cleaned other people's houses, I had many privileges denied to people of colour. Just my skin colour gives me advantages that people of other ethnicities don't enjoy.'

'That is indeed very unfair. What advantages do you have?'

'Ummm, well...education, jobs, opportunities, respect from patriarchal organisations. If you are black here, the odds are stacked against you. You cannot expect to get on in life.'

Dadafarin digested this thought for a moment. Not being black himself, he couldn't quite understand the relevance of the doctor's comments. 'So how does this affect me?' he enquired. 'After all, I am not black.'

'No, but you are foreign. Foreigners suffer many of the same injustices as black people. They are restricted in the jobs they can choose, the careers they can aspire to.'

'So acting is considered a profession of low social standing here?' Dadafarin asked, sounding surprised.

Dr Venngloss looked confused. 'Why do you say that?'

'It seems a lot of black and other minority people are on television. While I was watching television last night, during one period of advertisements, I only saw one white person.'

'Ah, but that is because we are fixing it. Black people are now being given more opportunities. We can only destroy inequality by forcing change. Equality can only come about with equity.'

Dadafarin had no idea what Dr Venngloss was talking about. 'Equity?' he enquired.

'Equity means adjusting systems so that they no longer discriminate. Forcing change, by elevating the disadvantaged, and removing power from the

privileged.'
'So those actors on the television advertisements are only given work because they are black?'

Dr Venngloss frowned. He could see he had much work to do. He turned to Dadafarin, looked him in the eyes. The doctor looked really tired. His eyes were a bit bloodshot and he had dark bags under his eyes.
'The only way to create equality is to abolish inequality' Dr Venngloss announced. 'It is only diversity, inclusion and equity that can create a fairer, more just world.'
Although he didn't quite understand what Dr Venngloss meant, he understood that this must be a profound statement. Dadafarin vowed to find out more about diversity, inclusion and equity, which seemed to please Dr Venngloss greatly. They made their way back to the hotel, where Dr Venngloss bumped elbows with him, promising to return within the next few days.

Dadafarin's fellow refugees seemed to spend the majority of their time talking in small groups, or taking selfies in the gardens to send to their friends back home and in the French refugee camps. Dadafarin had heard rumours that although they weren't supposed to leave the hotel, no-one would stop you if you did. Apparently, Noureldine and Ali had already walked into the local village twice, without being challenged when departing or returning to the hotel. Dadafarin wondered, however, how safe it was to leave the security of the hotel grounds.

Did any of his fellow asylum seekers realise that this country they were so pleased to be in was, in fact, not the land of dreams they had imagined, Dadafarin wondered? The idea of leaving the hotel grounds and risking being accosted by racists filled him with dread. Though he rarely spoke with any of his fellow guests, apart from brief greetings, a few of them would nod at him at breakfast, or as he passed them in the corridors. They all seemed to have got the message that he was not very sociable and, most of them being Muslim, probably had little in common with a Zoroastrian from Iran anyway.

The exception to this was Ibrahim, the tall, very dark-skinned young man from the Sudan, who always made a point of greeting Dadafarin whenever they came across each other. Ibrahim spoke excellent English, and Dadafarin decided he would like to get to know this bright and cheerful young man better. However, he found that his lack of social contact with the other refugees didn't bother him in the slightest. The online world was proving to be much more interesting.

IV
THE AWAKENING OF DADAFARIN

A short week after taking up residence in the Georgian Hotel, Dadafarin was surprised and pleased to receive a call from Carey, inviting him to attend a demonstration on the following Saturday with Dr Venngloss. The demonstration was in support of Black Lives Matter, a group campaigning against racism. Dadafarin had read a little about BLM online; initially, he had thought it was just a slogan. He had spent most of his first week in the hotel watching television, or browsing the internet on his new phone, trying to catch up on the rapidly changing political landscape of the Western world.

Dadafarin's fears, aroused by articles in The Sentinel, news reports on the BBC and his explorations on the internet, were confirmed by Dr Venngloss. Western civilisation was in crisis. It was nothing as Dadafarin had imagined. He had very quickly realised that if he was to make a success of his new life, he needed to become familiar with the new order of things, and quickly. Britain was turning out to be so different to his expectations that he sometimes wondered if he was in the right country. It seemed absolutely everything was tainted with racism, homophobia, transphobia and misogyny, along with several other long words that he hadn't yet found the meaning of.

Dr Venngloss had returned to visit twice, and they had walked in the beautiful and sunny hotel grounds for several hours. On one visit, Dr Venngloss gave Dadafarin a small pile of books to read. Dadafarin arranged these on the desk in his room, surprised that among them were a copy of the Communist Manifesto by Karl Marx and Frederich Engels. He had read this once before. Dadafarin had also been recommended a few YouTube channels via links sent in WhatsApp messages, mostly podcasts by political commentators. Soon YouTube themselves were suggesting other videos he might be interested in.

Dadafarin spent three days doing little apart from watching YouTube, except for attending meals and reading the newspaper. The receptionist, Claire, now kept him a copy of The Sentinel every morning, which he took to breakfast and then continued reading in the garden if it wasn't raining, or took back to his room if the weather was inclement. He also started following more people on Twitter, and, the more he followed, the more Twitter suggested.

Soon Dadafarin was following over fifty social justice warriors, a dozen or so celebrities, and several anarchists. He had yet to make his first tweet, as he was wary of opening himself up to being attacked, which seemed to be the main point of Twitter. The primary purpose of this strange form of social media, where you were restricted in how many characters you could write, seemed to be to enable you to find people whose opinions you disagreed with, and then be nasty to them. Dadafarin decided that he didn't really like Twitter. He couldn't really see the point in shouting at and insulting anyone who disagreed with you, even while trying to create a better world.

YouTube on the other hand turned out to be incredibly informative, with videos on everything from government cover-ups of UFO's, the search for a Covid vaccine being used as a front to develop injectable microchips that could be controlled through the new 5G phone network, to the mobilisation of hundreds of thousands of people in America and the UK to fight against systemic racism. Police seemed to be killing black people in America at an alarming rate. Donald Trump, the American President, was firmly on the side of white supremacy.

Examples of systemic racism were everywhere, and one YouTube video showed how the fascists were now cleverly resorting to micro-aggression to camouflage their bigotry. Micro-aggression could apparently be so subtle as to be indicated by a white person raising their eyebrows when a black person spoke. If white people acted like they were impressed by a black person's actions or words, this was, in fact, indicating that they were surprised at the black person's ability, or their grasp of a concept or idea. This was of course not just patronising, but downright racist.

Dadafarin watched one video on You-

Tube where two people, neither of whose sex he could work out, were arguing with a bald man over whether all women had vaginas. This did not make much sense to him, and sounded a bit gross, so he didn't watch the whole video. Another video he came across claimed that the Royal Family were in fact fascist lizards from another planet, which led to Dadafarin's growing suspicion that perhaps not everything on YouTube was completely true.

His days of watching television and YouTube and browsing Twitter left him feeling quite drained and pessimistic. How sad that a country he had always seen as a beacon of hope, freedom and unity had all along been hiding a dark secret, which was only now being exposed thanks to the selfless actions of those seeking social justice. He needed to understand this new world and it's peoples, all so different from his expectations, if he wished to thrive.

Their walks were the highlight of Dadafarin's week. Dr Venngloss seemed positively delighted at Dadafarin's evident interest in social justice. He proved able to absorb huge amounts of information, a trait that further endeared him to Dr Venngloss. The ideas of Critical Race Theory and intersectionality appeared to have already made a huge impact on this bright young man from a foreign culture.

During their third walk in the grounds, Dadafarin asked Dr Venngloss if his understanding of current society was correct. It seemed to him, he said, that the world was divided into perpetrators and victims, with victims having the most status. Victimhood appeared to depend on your place in a sort of network, or matrix, of identity. Identity was seemingly decided by the individual, though you didn't appear to be able to identify as another race. Dr Venngloss confirmed Dadafarin's hypotheses, though stressed that victimhood was not necessarily something to seek, but it was nothing to be ashamed of either.

One afternoon, they had a long discussion on this topic.

'Is it true', Dadafarin asked, 'that if, for example, you are black *and* transgender, that you are in fact blessed, like a saint?'

'Not quite. Victimhood is not a blessing' Dr Venngloss explained. 'Though being a victim does give you certain moral rights.'

'In that case, surely anyone wanting victimhood can just declare that they are gay, or transexual, or even something completely new?' Dadafarin posited as they wandered past the fish pond.

'Yes, that is a good point,' the Doctor said. 'though victimhood occurs due to the inherent racist and bigoted bias of society. It is not a goal, to be gained by deception. People who come out as gay or transexual, for example, are just acknowledging who they actually are rather than hiding in shame, as they were forced to do until very recently. And we should embrace that openness.'

'What exactly does systemic mean?' Dadafarin

asked. He'd seen and heard this word many times since his arrival in Britain.
'It means embedded in the system, for example through white supremacy.'
'What exactly is white supremacy?' Dadafarin asked.
'White supremacy is a social construct based on race, engineered to maintain power. Western society is built around it.'

Dadafarin thought on this for a few moments. 'So white people have constructed society entirely in their own image?'
'Exactly. And this has led to repression, colonisation, and the genocide of minorities, throughout known history.'
'And why has it taken so long for people to see the truth?'
'Ah, truth...' Dr Venngloss stopped walking as they passed under a huge oak tree, and turned towards Dadafarin. 'Truth is one of the casualties of white supremacy.'
'What do you mean, Dr Venngloss?'
Dr Venngloss explained, as they walked through the forest at the edge of the vast lawns, about truth. 'The traditional meaning of truth is also, in fact, just a white patriarchal social construct. What matters is *your* truth.'
'My truth?'
'Yes. Your lived experience. It's all very well saying, for example, that two plus two equals four. But if you were dyscalculic, which means unable to work

with numbers, two plus two might equal five. And then, for you, that is the truth.'
It all sounded a bit confusing, but very interesting. Dadafarin wondered how this would work in a practical context, for example civil engineering, but his brain was staring to hurt, so he suggested they get a coffee.

Dadafarin had by now learnt enough to know that he himself could identify as a victim. It could perhaps even help him to get asylum. It seemed that being persecuted bestowed you with certain privileges, not least among which seemed to be immunity from criticism. This realisation also made Dr Venngloss's dedication to this new way of thinking appear incredibly selfless. The unfortunate doctor inhabited no single recognised intersection on the complex matrix of identity: in fact, the only thing he had going for him was his allyship, a word that Dadafarin had first seen in The Sentinel. He had looked it up on Wikipedia.
"Allyship is the practice of emphasizing social justice, inclusion, and human rights by members of an ingroup, to advance the interests of an oppressed or marginalized outgroup" Wikipedia stated. Evidently, white people were the "ingroup." And although Dr Venngloss was evidently an ally, the original sin of whiteness would never leave him.

Dr Venngloss was also male, and apparently heterosexual, judging from the looks Dadafarin had seen him give two of the girls working in reception. Add to this his receding hairline and slight paunch, and you could see that Dr Venngloss was only a thought away from being a "gammon", the derogatory although evidently not racist term Dadafarin had seen directed at white men on Twitter, especially those who had voted for Brexit.

Dadafarin was extremely impressed by the sacrifices Dr Venngloss was prepared to make, to atone for the sin of being born to the wrong parents. Revelations about the inequality of British society only increased his respect for Dr Venngloss. Dr Venngloss was in fact, he realised, a living martyr. He was fully invested in an idea where he himself was the lowest denominator. Dadafarin could at least claim to occupy two points of intersection on the matrix of identity; he was both foreign, and of an obscure religion. Against him he had the fact that he was male, though it seemed for foreigners that their origin gave them certain exemptions from accusations of what he had seen called "toxic masculinity". He had realised this when he had come across an article in The Sentinel about child grooming in Rochdale.

A large group of men had been targeting underage girls in order to have sex with them. Although the men charged were obviously all of foreign origin, this was not mentioned at all in the article. It was only online, in an article in the Daily Post, that Dadafarin had discovered that all the accused men were Muslims, and that the police had ignored reports of their activities for years, out of fear of being accused of Islamophobia.

Another interesting fact Dadafarin had gleaned from the newspaper, breakfast time television and the BBC was that any amount of African blood in your ancestry, no matter how little, meant you were actually black, irrespective of your features and skin colour. Dadafarin had been quite surprised to discover that Prince Harry's wife Meghan, although Mediterranean in appearance, was in fact black. So too was Colin Kaepernick, the light-skinned NFL star who first took kneeling into the public consciousness. In spite of being mixed race, and being brought up by white foster parents in a white neighbourhood, Colin's blackness had never left him, causing him such agonies that he decided to kneel when the American anthem was being played before an important match. The video had gone viral, and now kneeling was viewed as an important and symbolic way to signal your fealty to the anti-racism struggle.

On Twitter, anyone identifying as black, or any other of the bewildering array of minority identities, appeared to be able to say anything they wanted, whereas their fascist critics were soon silenced under an avalanche of comments highlighting their bigotry. Many of those attacked subsequently got banned from Twitter, including the current President of the USA, Donald Trump. During their talks, Dadafarin had to frequently interrupt to ask Dr Venngloss to explain specific words and phrases, such as "social construct", "cisgender" and many others. The world was finally waking up to the inequities of history, and he was lucky enough to be witnessing first-hand the rise of a wonderful new, fairer world. He couldn't wait to get into London and see this being put into action.

V
IN THE BELLY OF THE BEAST: A TRIP TO LONDON

Dadafarin woke up on the Saturday morning of his trip to London with a strange feeling of enthusiasm mixed with trepidation. He had still not left the hotel grounds since his arrival, and was not sure what to expect. However, he had utmost faith in Dr Venngloss, and was excited to finally have the opportunity to see social justice in action. Lockdown was still in force, but Dr Venngloss assured Dadafarin that protests, though perhaps not strictly allowed, were tolerated. This verified the conclusion Dadafarin had come to after watching footage from Bristol and another demonstration in London on the same day. Some things were evidently far more important than a pandemic from China.

The good doctor arrived at ten in the morning on the Saturday to find Dadafarin waiting for him in reception. As they drove towards London in Dr Venngloss's old and slightly smelly Citroen, littered with discarded take-away containers and sweet wrappers, Dr Venngloss gave him a quick heads-up on where they were going. They were heading to central London, which Dadafarin now knew to be not just where the Queen lived and Parliament sat, but it was also the power centre of the white capitalist patriarchy who controlled the country. However, London had a very progressive mayor, Sadia Cant, himself from immigrant stock, who supported BLM.

As they drove through a battered and decrepit housing estate where a group of white youths stood around a burning car, Dr Venngloss told Dadafarin more about white privilege. The Western system of democracy, science and social structure had been designed and built by white people, entirely in their own image. The very buildings themselves were symbols of white supremacy, designed by their grandeur to cow foreigners into submission. If black people showed resentment against white people, this had to be seen in the context of the hundreds of years of oppression they had been and still were subject to. White people were so conditioned into white supremacy that they didn't even realise that they were all racist.

'So you too are a racist?' Dadafarin asked, surprised.

'I am trying my best not to be' the good doctor replied, sighing. 'I have to be vigilant.'

Dadafarin already knew that the demonstration they were to attend was in response to the racist killing in America of a well-respected petty criminal named George Floyd. George had a history of violent assault and drug abuse, but was in the process of turning his life around when he had been killed by a policeman kneeling on his neck for just over nine minutes. The policeman's three colleagues stood around and did nothing as George Floyd was suffocated in public view on a Minneapolis street. George had been violently arrested for the trivial crime of using counterfeit money in a convenience store. Dadafarin had seen the video on TV and on YouTube, and it was a very harrowing clip. The policeman appeared to Dadafarin to be totally incompetent, and probably a bit scared of the man he was arresting. His colleagues were evidently complicit by their inaction.

Dadafarin had been shocked to find out that the cop who killed George Floyd was a racist, in spite of having a wife who came from Laos. Perhaps his choice of wife had been a form of cultural appropriation? Dr Venngloss explained that all police in America and Britain were racist, even the black ones, who were “white adjacent”. It was all part of the evils of systemic racism, now thankfully recognised as the main cause of all humanities problems, from poverty to climate change. It had tragically taken the murder of an innocent man to bring it to public attention. America had erupted in protest at the killing of George Floyd, unleashing years of pent-up emotion, possibly aggravated by the pandemic, and now it was Britain's turn to reject white supremacy.

Driving through a tatty looking area on the outskirts of London, Dr Venngloss became quite animated as he explained that the only way to stop systemic racism was by defunding the police, paying reparations for the sins of historic slavery, destroying capitalism and abolishing the patriarchal nuclear family. His evident passion on the subject nearly caused him to hit a parked lorry. Checking his seatbelt again, Dadafarin told Dr Venngloss that he had recently read about all this, when he had followed a link to a BLM UK GoFundMe page from the comments section on a YouTube video. He hadn't quite understood what a nuclear family was, but assumed it was a reference to white men having developed atomic weapons, that most abominable of all man's inventions. Nodding enthusiastically, Dr Venngloss continued his monologue, explaining that if real change meant destroying the whole corrupt structure of society in the process, that was a small price to pay. The only way to achieve a better world was by burning down the old one. Seemingly now spent, he slumped back and to Dadafarin's relief became absorbed in driving.

Dadafarin reflected on the fact that just a mere few weeks earlier he had imagined Britain to be a model of contemporary free society. How quickly things can change when people wake up to injustice, he thought to himself. On YouTube, he had recently seen some videos from Portland, in America. In their fight against racism, the citizens of Portland, who in the 2010 census were shown as being 76% white, were so incensed by systemic racism that every night they took to the streets to burn down police stations, loot capitalist shops, and harass other white people, or any blacks who were not really black, for failing to stand up to racism, patriarchy, capitalism and central government. This continued protesting was working; many of the police had resigned, the Mayor was now supporting the protestors, and capitalism in Portland was failing as shops burned and businesses closed.

Just outside London, they left the car in a side street, and Dr Venngloss called a pre-arranged taxi on his mobile phone. It was initially very quiet on the way into the city. However, as they got closer to Trafalgar Square, it was obvious something big was happening. Crowds of people were filtering through the streets, many holding placards. Dr Venngloss told Dadafarin that Trafalgar Square, where they were heading, had been named in honour of the battle that the narcissistic imperialist Admiral Nelson had won against the French or Spanish or someone a few centuries ago. Nelson had been gay, but you didn't find this in the history books. Being gay, apart from being an offence punishable by hanging in those days, didn't fit the colonial narrative. Instead, they celebrated his militaristic devotion to Empire. Erecting a statue celebrating the defeat of foreigners just showed how racist the whole system had always been.

As they got closer to the city centre, the streets started filling with people, many waving banners and shouting. Soon there were so many people heading towards the demonstration that they had to pay off the taxi driver and join the throngs winding through the streets. Dadafarin looked at the placards and banners carried by the crowds. Many had Black Lives Matter written on them in large letters. Dadafarin had already seen this banner many times on television and YouTube, and it was currently the most popular hashtag on Twitter, but he asked Dr Venngloss to explain exactly what it meant. Was it just a slogan, as The Sentinel claimed, or was there an organised group behind it? BLM UK had a GoFundMe page, after all.

'It is a hashtag, and has been adopted as a rallying cry for a group of like-minded individuals, coming together to effect change. The organisation of BLM as a group was necessary to organise demonstrations and create awareness. Black people have been downtrodden for centuries, here and abroad. America was built on slavery and genocide. BLM's aim is to show that black people's lives matter, and to highlight all the injustices they have been subjected to historically, and which are still ongoing in contemporary society.'

'Don't all lives matter?' Dadafarin asked. A couple dressed in Lycra, both of indeterminate sex, one with shocking pink hair, overheard him and very quickly became aggressive.

'Fucking Nazi scum!' one shouted, and made as if to strike Dadafarin.

Dr Venngloss quickly stepped in and explained to the snarling pink youth. 'My friend is a refugee from Iran. He is here to join our demands for just-

ice.'
The couple backed off, muttering suspiciously. 'Tell him to mind his language!'

Dr Venngloss pulled Dadafarin away, and they continued towards the sounds of shouting. Some placards read “White Silence is Violence” and “Hands Up, Don't Shoot”, although none of the police at the edge of the square seemed to be armed. Dadafarin looked around to see if there were any snipers positioned on rooftops. If so, they were well hidden.

On entering Trafalgar square, Dadafarin was surprised at quite how many people there were.
'Is it safe for so many people to be on the streets?' he asked. 'Surely such a large gathering will spread Covid?'
'Some things are more important' Dr Venngloss replied. 'It is our time. Justice is on our side.'

At the edge of the square, a number of smiling police knelt down in front of a group of shouting demonstrators. Most, but not all, of the protesters wore masks. Many seemed far more interested in taking selfies or filming the crowd than taking part. Some protestors were dressed completely in black, wore balaclavas or scarves covering everything except their eyes, which struck Dadafarin as very public minded. No germs would get through those. They must be really hot though, he thought; he was sweating, and he was only wearing jeans and a T-shirt. A small group of people dressed entirely in black were erecting barricades across the square. A young man waved a flag showing the letter A in a circle from a perch on one of the lions. Everyone seemed very angry.

What impressed Dadafarin the most was the overwhelming number of people of obviously Caucasian extraction, keen to atone for their sin of whiteness. As in Portland, white people here were evidently ashamed of their skin colour. What humility they displayed! A young black woman in dark military fatigues stood on a makeshift stage with a megaphone, calling the crowd to action and pumping a gloved fist in the air. Dadafarin couldn't understand anything she was shouting, apart from “Black Power!”, repeated every time the crowd's enthusiasm seemed to be waning. The crowd obviously loved this, raising fists and joining in the chants.

After his initial reservations about this new Britain, Dadafarin now fully understood what they were fighting for. Surely this was the best of all possible worlds? The downtrodden were now asserting their rights, and the oppressors put in their place. What a brave new world! Dadafarin felt a warm rush of excitement and happiness course through him. He had finally found a place that would celebrate his differences, instead of shunning him. To add to his delight, they spied Carey in the crowd talking to several large black men, some with dreadlocks, dressed in paramilitary-style costumes.

VI
WHAT BECAME OF DADAFARIN AND DR VENNGLOSS AMONG THE SOCIAL JUSTICE WARRIORS

Carey greeted Dadafarin warmly and introduced him to her companions, who didn't seem to be very interested in him. They appeared to be far more interested in the tight tank top Carey was wearing, the word LOVE written across it in a large multi-coloured font. The effect on them of this wonderful word spread across her breast was delightful to behold. A sense of purpose flowed through the air, like the delightful whiff of lavender in the hotel gardens, infecting everyone with joy and a feeling of unity. The whole crowd was gripped by an energy the likes of which Dadafarin had never witnessed before.

After wishing the men well, Carey joined the two friends as they headed towards the large crowds gathered around Nelson's Column. The crowd here were resorting to more direct means of protest than waving placards and chanting. Dadafarin was very impressed with the police. They just stood and smiled as the demonstrators threw bottles and any other objects they could find at them, sprayed statues, smashed a few shop windows on the periphery of the square, and, from an electrical store down a side road, made off with televisions, stereos, and even a washing machine, presumably to give to the needy.

It seemed that the Defund the Police hashtag campaign Dadafarin had seen on Twitter had already paid dividends, though perhaps not quite in the way intended. In addition to it's stated objective of transferring investment in the police to investment in the community, it also appeared to have made the police ill-equipped to do their job. The only weapons they seemed permitted to use were smiles. The police had neither guns nor water cannon; they weren't even firing tear gas at the crowds. Maybe that's why the police seemed so friendly, Dadafarin thought. However, taking the knee was surely a sham on the part of law enforcement officials. If not, why did social justice warriors hate them so much?

A large group of white men suddenly appeared from a side street, several wearing football shirts, some with no shirts at all. Many were covered in tattoos that had used so much ink that it was impossible to decipher them. In fact, seeing a mess of jumbled colour on one man's arm, Dadafarin at first thought someone had been sick on him. They were evidently all drunk, and started hurling abuse at the protesters. The police suddenly swung into action, trying to keep the rival groups apart. Bottles, stones, flares and insults flew through the air. Very quickly it became apparent to Dadafarin that this new group weren't very happy about black lives mattering. As Dadafarin later found out, they were football supporters, recruited by the fascist thug Timmy Rogerton to travel to London to protect white imperialist statues and monuments from being damaged by the social justice warriors. One of these men appeared later on the news, urinating on a memorial he was protecting. The police tried to keep the two groups apart, but with limited success. They seemed to be less restrained when dealing with the football supporters than they were with the BLM protesters. Several police retired from the fray with blood pouring from wounds, a police woman was thrown from her horse, and the three friends decided it was time to leave.

They joined a group of people marching towards Hyde Park, where an actor from Star Wars was apparently going to speak to the crowd. Dadafarin had noticed on Twitter and in the news that people from Hollywood seemed to really have their finger on the pulse when it came to social injustice. What better qualifications are there to have than achieving fame and fortune in society in spite of all the barriers placed there by the white patriarchy? The stars of Hollywood were truly an inspiration.

Their route took them past Parliament Square, where a statue of Winston Churchill stood. Large amounts of people were gathered here, too. Dadafarin was impressed to see some men in uniform, who Dr Venngloss explained were military veterans, standing in front of Winston Churchill's statue. The crowd seemed to sense that attacking this statue while these men stood at attention in front of it was not acceptable, and an uneasy truce seemed to be in force.

As they left the square, Dr Venngloss smiled at a group of youths busy pulling up flagstones. Most of them were white, but evidently they were all social justice warriors, as they were being supervised by a very well-built black man wearing a paramilitary uniform. It was wonderful to behold, people of different races, working in harmony. One of the white youths, a scrawny little man with a ferret-like face, seemed to take a sudden dislike to Dr Venngloss. He walked over, and, with one punch, sent Dr Venngloss sprawling on the floor. 'Gammon scum!' he snarled, kicking Dr Venngloss in the ribs. This seemed to precipitate several other demonstrators to join in, and before Carey and Dadafarin could react, three men and a woman were all kicking and stamping on poor Dr Venngloss, who was lying curled up on the floor in a foetal position.

'Run!' screamed Dr Venngloss. Grabbing Dadafarin's hand, Carey ran towards an alleyway leading out of the square and they made their escape, the screams of Dr Venngloss ringing in their ears.

Dadafarin's last view of Dr Venngloss was of him standing unsteadily, attempting to fend off two youths who were circling him, one holding a bottle.

'Shouldn't we help him?' Dadafarin asked Carey, as they stopped, panting, to get their breath on the

next street.
'No', Carey replied. 'Once all this anger is triggered, it's best not to interfere. We don't know what made them angry. They were BLM supporters, not football hooligans. I really don't know what happened. The police will help him.' At that, she burst into tears, and Dadafarin gathered her in his arms, comforting her as he felt her tears wetting his shirt. He could smell her perfume, floral and fresh, and also the smell of shampoo on her hair. He was getting an erection, and hoped she didn't notice.

After Carey ceased crying, they continued to Hyde Park, which was crowded with protesters. They arrived just in time to hear John Boyega from Star Wars make a rousing speech to a rapt audience, most of whom seemed to prefer watching Mr Boyega on their 'phone screens him rather than directly. The crowd appeared less agitated here, and mostly stood silently, phones recording, as John Boyega made his inspiring speech. Especially poignant was his statement that “I need you to understand how painful it is to be reminded every day that your race means nothing, and that isn't the case any more, that was never the case any more.” It was so moving that even John Boyega himself was in tears. The crowd erupted in a frenzy of chants and cheers. Carey stood in rapt admiration, and Dadafarin realised he was falling in love with her. He wondered what had become of Dr Vennglos s.

VII
MEETING MARTIN

After John Boyega's rousing speech, people started making their way out of the park. Dadafarin became separated from Carey as a sudden surge of the crowd took them in opposite directions. She mouthed something as she was borne away, but Dadafarin could not make it out. He fought his way to the edge of the milling crowd and found a bench, on which was sitting a bearded old white man dressed in very scruffy clothes clutching something in a brown paper bag. Did this man really have privilege, Dadafarin wondered? It didn't look like he was enjoying it much. Dadafarin sat down and took stock of his position. He realised he had no idea where he was, or indeed where the hotel was. He also had no money, and after patting his pockets he realised he had lost his mobile phone, or perhaps had it pick-pocketed.

The old man turned to Dadafarin and asked 'Are you one of those snowflakes?'

Dadafarin was confused. Was this some surreal British attempt at humour? It reminded him of something he'd seen from an old show called Monty Python a few days earlier, while flicking through channels on the TV.

'Snowflake? No, I'm a raindrop!' Dadafarin replied, laughing at his own witticism. The old man looked at him in apparent disgust, slid to the farther end of the bench and stood up, clutching his brown paper bag. He gave Dadafarin a furtive look before wandering off, muttering to himself.

Dadafarin stood up and wandered to the edge of the park. Across the road, he saw what he recognised from postcards he'd seen of London as an underground train station. He crossed the road at some traffic lights and wandered towards the station, unsure of how to find out about trains, and with no means to pay for one. He suddenly realised he didn't even know where to catch a train to even if he could pay for it. He felt vulnerable, and very alone.

Outside the station a young man was playing what sounded like jazz on a trumpet. He had long brown hair topped with a multi-coloured wool hat, and a stringy goatee beard. A plain blue cardigan with several holes in it over a dirty white T-shirt, combat trousers and old army boots indicated that this enterprising young man was likely reliant on his public performances for food. A Costbucks Coffee cup on the pavement in front of him contained a few paltry coins. He looked a kind and harmless soul, so Dadafarin listened for a while, and when the man stopped playing, approached him.

'Hello? Excuse me, I am lost. I need to get to the Georgian Hotel, in Kent, but I don't know how, and I don't have any money.'

'Hotel? You're staying in an hotel, and you don't have any money?'

'Yes. No. I mean..' Dadafarin laughed nervously. 'I am not from here. I am from Iran'
'Iran?'
Dadafarin explained his circumstances to the young man, who introduced himself as Martin.
'I am Dada', Dadafarin introduced himself.
'Really? Cool name. Is it for real?'
'It is short for Dadafarin, which means Born of Justice' Dadafarin explained proudly. Martin seemed very impressed. He told Dadafarin he had been at the protest earlier, and was now trying to make a little bit of money before returning home. There was a party later, and he wanted to buy some drinks to take with him.
'But, never mind, I've got enough now anyway', Martin said. 'Why don't you come back to my place? We'll see if we can work out how to get you home.'

It turned out that Martin lived fairly close by, in a very grand house fronted with columns that reminded Dadafarin of the fire temple in Yazd. Set back from the road, it was five storeys high, at the end of a line of connected houses making up a large crescent. There was apparently something wrong with the front door, because they entered via means of the kitchen window, around the back of the house. A wooden box provided a step to make ingress easier. Inside was a large kitchen, lined with wooden panels, with a long blonde marble counter top, a huge silver refrigerator built into one wall. Martin filled an electric kettle.

'Tea?'

'Yes, thank you' Dadafarin replied. He knew that drinking tea was an important social ritual in England, and felt truly honoured to be invited to take part. 'Your house is beautiful' Dadafarin continued, as Martin took milk out of the refrigerator. 'It reminds me of home.'

Martin stopped what he was doing and looked at Dadafarin with new interest.

'You lived in a house like this?'

“No' Dadafarin smiled. 'Not at all. The front of your house looks like Yazd Atash Behram, a fire temple in my home city. It holds one of the nine Atash Behram's, the highest grade of fire. Thinking of it makes me miss home.'

'Fire Temple? How cool. You worship fire?'

'Not exactly.' Dadafarin was interrupted by the arrival of a young woman, very thin, dressed in a loose-fitting cotton dress and barefoot. Martin introduced her as Kyla. Kyla seemed a bit distracted, and, after pausing at the sink, which was full of dirty dishes, she darted out of the room again.

Passing Dadafarin his tea, Martin offered him a biscuit and then suggested they sit somewhere more comfortable. 'Let's sit in the lounge.'

Dadafarin picked up his tea and followed Martin into a long hallway.

'Living here is a protest against capitalism' Martin announced, looking back at Dadafarin. 'Five of us live here usually. Sometimes we have parties.'

They seemed to have rather an ironic take on protest, living in an evidently very expensive house, yet simultaneously showing their disdain for the baubles of the rich. In the hallway, circles had been painted round the eyes of a stern looking gentleman in an oil painting in the hall, and a large letter A had been drawn on his coat. Dadafarin had seen this symbol painted on a statue earlier in the day. In the lounge, which was furnished with large, dark brown leather couches, the letter A in a circle appeared again, next to a slogan painted in red letters saying "Sometimes Antisocial. Always Antifascist.". A torn poster that Dadafarin recognised as being of Che Guevara hung at an angle on the wall above a dark grand piano on which a man dressed only in a pair of shorts lay smoking cannabis, judging by the smell.

'What does the letter A mean?' Dadafarin asked Martin. Martin seemed rather surprised that Dadafarin did not recognise the symbol.

'Antifascist. We are dedicated to fighting fascism' Martin replied. 'But some people say it means anarchy. Same thing, really.'

'Where do you go to fight fascism?' Dadafarin asked, thinking that they must be globe-trotting revolutionaries. Judging by Martin's house, they could evidently afford it. Martin laughed.

'Where? Everywhere, of course. Fascism is everywhere. Tonight we're fighting fascism. Come along and see. We'll get you home tomorrow. Chill out a bit'. He grabbed the cannabis cigarette from the

man on the piano, and offered it to Dadafarin.
'No, thanks. I don't smoke that stuff. You shouldn't either. It's illegal.'
Martin laughed. 'Yes, it's illegal. Which makes it even better'. He took a huge puff, coughed, and passed it back to the man on the piano, who now sat up, his bare legs dangling. Martin introduced him to Dadafarin.
'Whip, this is Dada. He's from Iran. He worships fire. His name means Born of Justice.'
'Awesome, Dude!' The man jumped down off the piano. He quite short and wiry, with very short hair and an intense look in dark eyes. He grabbed Dadafarin's hand and pumped it enthusiastically. 'Awesome!' he said again.
'Dada, this is Whip' They shook hands. In spite of his small stature, Whip had an air of quiet menace about him. He had a very firm handshake, and stared hard into Dadafarin's eyes at they clasped hands.
'Cool name, dude' Whip said. Everyone seemed to comment on his name, which always made Dadafarin feel quite proud.

Martin sat down at the piano and played a short bit of classical music that Dadafarin recognised, but couldn't put a name to. Martin was evidently a very accomplished musician, and Dadafarin couldn't help wondering why he was dressed like a tramp and busking outside tube stations, when he was obviously wealthy and talented. He'd heard of English eccentricity; perhaps Martin was a genuine eccentric Lord? When Martin finished playing, they went back to the kitchen for more tea, sitting round a large rectangular oak table, the top of which was roughly inscribed with the symbol Dadafarin now knew to be that of the antifascists. Whip continually rolled large cannabis cigarettes, which they referred to as 'spliffs', sharing them with Martin. They found a can of beer for Dadafarin, and then Whip told him more about fascism in Britain, and how the police were its agents. Dadafarin listened in horror as Whip told him what was really going on in Britain, and, in fact, the whole Western world.

Whip explained that the police all belonged to an organisation called the Freemasons, who were in turn part of a secretive organisation that was seeking to take over the entire planet. This cabal could trace its roots right back to the Knights Templar, a sect of fascist warrior monks from over 1000 years ago. It seemed Bill Gates, the man who started Microsoft, was one of the kingpins. He had invested in vaccine laboratories years before Covid 19 had appeared; wasn't that a convenient coincidence? Behind all this, Whip told Dadafarin, was a secret organisation called the WEF, the World Economic Forum. They were currently implementing a program called the Great Reset. The lockdowns were in fact the first stage of their plan to establish a world government, get rid of all money, and force people to live on insects. While the Great Reset appeared to be socialist in outlook, it was in fact just another form of fascism. It relied on elites controlling the population, which was obviously not compatible with anarchist ideals. Soon, there would be a "vaccine" (Whip made the sign of inverted commas when he said this), and the next stage would begin. The government planned to implant electronic chips in the entire population, using the vaccine programme as cover, so they could track them using the new 5G phone network.

Dadafarin had seen two videos on YouTube saying exactly the same things, so was not at all surprised by Whip's claims. 'So why don't they just track people's mobile phones?' he asked Whip.

'They get more information with the chip. You can't leave it at home or switch it off like you can a mobile phone' Whip explained. 'And, on the second vaccination, they will implant a device that can alter your DNA.' This was truly shocking to Dadafarin. How had the world come to this? It certainly needed to be stopped.

'So, you are both against fascists, but what are you *for?* Dadafarin asked Martin.

'For? We are for destroying fascism, in all it's forms' Martin replied, sipping his tea.

'But what then?'

'Then? There is no then. The battle will never be over' Whip interjected.

'Do you not have a plan for afterwards?'

'Afterwards?' Martin said, fingering his wispy goatee. 'Why think about afterwards when we still have to think about today? Afterwards is for other people to worry about. For us, now is all that matters.' On this note, Martin went to the kitchen to make more tea.

Later, Kyla cooked a bland insipid stew from lentils and some unidentifiable vegetables, which Dadafarin ate not just out of politeness, but also because he hadn't eaten since breakfast. As they ate, Whip gave a brief description of the new society he envisaged, belying his earlier comments about the revolution never being finished. The population of his free society would govern by form of committees, and everyone would have a say in every major governmental decision. Dadafarin's query as to how this society would not get completely bogged down in bureaucracy went unanswered, as ultimately did his confusion over why an anarchist would want a different form of government.

'Surely anarchy means no government at all?' Dadafarin asked.

'Government by the people is not government' Whip explained, rolling a huge joint as Kyla cleared the table. Passing Kyla his empty plate, Dadafarin was a bit surprised to find traditional gender roles still being followed by progressive revolutionaries.

'There will be no elected officials' Whip continued, taking a large puff and passing the joint to Martin. 'Representatives will be chosen by the people at a local level. They in turn elect one of their number to represent their committee at the macro level. And so on.'

Dadafarin was confused. He was not really sure Whip had thought all this through properly, but he said nothing. It all sounded suspiciously like Marxism. Whip called it Democratic Anarchy. With a final flourish, Whip licked the joint, flicked it into his lips, and lit it from a Zippo that he he then snapped shut with a loud crack, all in one obviously well practised move.
'Time to party' Martin announced.

VIII
DADAFARIN PARTIES WITH THE ANTI-FASCISTS

Outside, the sun had gone down, a soft twilight greeting them as they made their way out of the window and round the side of the house to the street. Kyla said goodbye to the three men. She was going to a Vegan recipe swap meeting, so couldn't accompany them. Kyla hugged the two anti-fascists and gave Dadafarin a peck on the cheek as she said goodbye. The three friends walked towards the tube station where Dadafarin had met Martin, Dadafarin feeling quite excited about attending his first party in Britain.

The party was in Brixton, Martin told Dadafarin. Dadafarin had heard of Brixton before; it was famous for producing some great bands, notably Hot Chocolate, whom his mother had often played on her small gramophone. He also knew Brixton to be the home of lots of Rastafarians, a group he felt some affinity to, them being another minority religion struggling for survival. Dadafarin and his new friends caught the tube to Brixton, jumping the turnstiles (to stop capitalists profiting off what should be free public transport, according to Whip), then made their way to a small street named Overton Road. Martin seemed very amused by the road's name, pointing to a sign on the side of a house.

'We're going through the Overton Window!' he exclaimed, and both Whip and him cheered.
'What is the Overton Window?' Dadafarin asked.
'The Overton Window is the range of policies politically acceptable to the public at any given time' Martin explained. 'It's shifting, and tonight, we're going to move it a little more.' This caused another giggling fit from the two anti-fascists. The whole street was packed with revellers. People had evidently come from far and wide, and, in common with the demonstrators, didn't seem to be observing any social distancing at all. In common with demonstrations, it appeared that street parties did not spread Covid.

The party was already in full swing when the three friends arrived. Martin and Whip had dressed completely in black for the occasion, and had given Dadafarin a rather smelly balaclava, telling him to 'keep it handy'. Quite what for, he wasn't sure, as it was a very warm evening. Huge sound systems boomed out rap music, and a diverse, multi-ethnic crowd gyrated in the street, most seemingly very drunk. The sickly-sweet fug of cannabis smoke wafted through the air.

Someone thrust a beer into Dadafarin's hand, and then Martin and Whip pulled him away and towards a commotion further up the road, where Dadafarin could see flashing blue lights. Pink smoke from flares mixed with flashing blue smoke above the police vehicles, creating a throbbing purple smog over a group of young men and several women dressed in black, who were throwing bricks at a line of police with riot shields. The air was full of shouts, sirens, and the pulsing beat of the music. One police vehicle was on fire, while a young man danced on its roof. A garden wall had been demolished to provide ammunition, and Dadafarin even saw a small model of a deformed man being thrown at the police lines.

The noise was deafening. As they approached the line of police, Whip ripped off his shirt and headed screaming into the melee, all the veins on his arms standing out as he roared in defiance, and then he disappeared in a tangle of bodies and riot shields. Martin grabbed Dadafarin's arm, pulling him towards a makeshift barricade, behind which several Antifa revellers were huddled. The protestors were picking up bricks and lobbing them in the general direction of the police, then crouching down again.

'This is the party I came for' said Martin. Picking up a brick in each hand, Martin jumped over the barricade and headed towards a police van. He evaded one policeman with a deft body-swerve and managed to throw both bricks at the van, one starring the windscreen through its protective mesh cover, the other bouncing off the side of the van and hitting a policeman. Two other policemen charged Martin from the side, bringing him down in a heap on the road.

Dadafarin stood up, and immediately felt something smack into his right leg. He collapsed, a wave of pain from his leg making him unable to stand, then three policemen were on him. They handcuffed his hands behind him as he lay face down on the road, pulled him roughly to his feet, then marched him to a van. Dadafarin was relieved to see Martin sat among several other young men in the back of the van. Martin's face was covered in blood from a cut above his left eye. He winked at Dadafarin as he sat down next to him. 'We showed the bastards, hey?'

IX
DR VENNGLOSS AND THE SHIRT OF SHAME

Dadafarin and Martin were taken to a nearby police station, where they were searched, finger-printed, then locked in separate cells. Dadafarin was placed in a cell with three other men, none of whom had been in the police van. One was an old man who appeared very drunk, the other two were young white men dressed in black, who looked like they could be brothers. Both had short brown hair, blue eyes and looked very tough. Dadafarin guessed they were from Antifa. One of them asked Dadafarin why he'd been arrested.
'I am not sure' Dadafarin replied. 'I was at a party in Brixton.' He explained that he was a refugee, and had only been trying to get back to his hotel. He asked if anyone had a phone, so he could try and call Dr Venngloss. However, they had all had their phones removed, save the drunk, who didn't own one. Dadafarin wasn't sure he could remember Dr Venngloss's number anyway.

The cell was small, furnished only with a single bed with a foul-looking dirty blanket on it, a metal toilet with no seat in one corner. It turned out that the drunk old man had spent the previous night there. The other occupants had arrived shortly before Dadafarin. It was now around 11pm, and Dadafarin wondered whether he would be given his own cell. While leaning against the wall as far as he could get from the blocked toilet, he discovered that the two young men were indeed Antifa, and had also been arrested at the party. When they found out he was a refugee, they assured him that he would be released in the morning, as refugees were known to be exempt from the law.

One of the men, Max, kept asking him about Iran, and then asked whether it was true that they executed homosexuals.

'Oh yes' Dadafarin answered, 'They execute anyone they don't like. That's why I left'

'Are you gay?' the other man asked.

'Oh no, not me. It's a sin' Dadafarin replied. 'Though perhaps killing them is taking things a bit far' he added, in case they thought he was homophobic.

The two men looked at each other, then Max asked him about his political views.

'I support the freedom of the common man. I like how fair the British are. You can say anything you like, as long as you don't offend anyone. I think democracy is a wonderful thing.'

'Democracy is the road to socialism' Max said.

'Karl Marx said that' Dadafarin replied.

'You've read Marx?' The two men looked at each other, Max raising his eyebrows. Even the old man seemed impressed.

'Yes, I've read some of his writing. He seems quite popular here in Britain.'

Before they could press him further, a policeman opened the door of the cell, flanked by two other officers wearing riot gear, and called out Dadafarin's name.

'That is me' Dadafarin shouted, and made his way towards them. The policeman with the keys ushered him out of the cell and locked the door behind them. Dadafarin was then led down a narrow corridor to the main police office, where several tired-looking police men and women were drinking coffee. Several of them had bruises on their faces, and one had a black eye.

Dadafarin was led into an office adjacent to the main desk, where an old man with a bandage round his head, and his left arm in plaster, rose from a chair in front of a desk full of papers.

'Dada!' the old man exclaimed, in a familiar voice. 'It is so good to see you!' He pulled off his black face mask, and, with a shock of recognition, Dadafarin realised that this old, battered man was none other than Dr Venngloss! He looked several years older, had several scabs on his face, and held his plastered arm away from his body, as if it pained him. He walked towards Dadafarin, and awkwardly embraced him with his one good arm.

'Dr Venngloss!' What happened to you?'

'Never mind that. Let's just get you out of here' he replied. 'This is Lesley', Dr Venngloss continued, gesturing towards a slight young man sitting in a chair, who Dadafarin had not at first noticed. Was this the same Lesley who was the lawyer in his asylum case, he wondered? Dr Venngloss had mentioned Lesley several times.

As Lesley stood up, Dadafarin was no longer sure he was a man. He could possibly be a she. Lesley had quite soft features, and appeared to be wearing eye shadow. Short blonde hair framed a clear skinned round face, the lower half covered by an orange mask, blue eyes sparkling in the fluorescent light. 'Lesley works with me. They are handling the legal side of your asylum application' Dr Venngloss continued. 'They are very experienced in immigration law.' Dadafarin looked around the office for another person, but couldn't see anyone else. Yet Dr Venngloss seemed to be referring to more than one person. Dadafarin was confused, but kept quiet. He felt a little ashamed at the good doctor finding him in trouble with the police, and just wanted to get back to his room in the hotel.

After being cautioned by the police for his part in the party, and given a slice of cake to take away with him, it being the custody officers birthday, Dadafarin was released. Dr Venngloss gave his personal assurances to the police that Dadafarin would remain in his hotel from now on, and he was free once more. Outside, they climbed into a small bright orange car which smelt of perfume. Lesley drove, and Dr Venngloss joined Dadafarin in the back.

'What about my friend Martin?' Dadafarin asked as they drove off. 'Shouldn't we try and get him released?'

'I am sure he will be fine' Dr Venngloss reassured him. 'They normally release protestors without charge.'

On the way back to the hotel, they exchanged their news. Dr Venngloss had been rescued by some football supporters, evidently thinking, as his attackers seemingly had, that he was one of them.

'But why did the protesters think you were a football supporter?' asked Dadafarin.

'Ah, well, that was my fault entirely' Dr Venngloss explained. 'Did you notice the shirt I was wearing?' Dadafarin vaguely remembered a pale yellow shirt, but couldn't be sure.

'That shirt was made by a company called Ben Sherman' the good doctor continued. 'Ben Sherman shirts are much favoured by fascists, and I knew that, so it was entirely my fault that they attacked me. My daughter gave me the shirt for my birthday, and, not wanting to offend her, I kept it. In fact, I should have pointed out her error, and destroyed the shirt.'

There seemed to be many traps and pitfalls on the road to social justice, Dadafarin thought to himself. One really had to be careful.

After being rescued, Dr Venngloss explained, he had made his way to the local hospital. An X-ray had shown that his arm was broken, but apart from that and several cuts and bruises, he had been very lucky. Dadafarin then told Dr Venngloss about his time with the anti-fascists,

and how he had come to be arrested.
'You are lucky they didn't actually see you throw bricks, or cause damage' Dr Venngloss admonished Dadafarin. You must avoid Antifa. While they have noble aims, their methods, do, shall we say, tend towards the extreme? You cannot afford to be caught breaking the law. It would needlessly complicate your asylum claim.'
'But weren't we breaking the law by going to the protest?' Dadafarin enquired, looking confused.
'Ah well, you see, not really, no. We weren't engaged in violence. We were peacefully campaigning for social justice. That's completely different.' Dr Venngloss then went on to inform Dadafarin that he had a screening interview, in relation to his asylum application, on the following Tuesday. Normally, he would have to go to Croydon in London. 'But, as there are several of you, and due to the pandemic, you will be interviewed at the hotel. Lesley will prepare you for the interview.'

Back at the hotel, Dr Venngloss said goodbye, hugging Dadafarin again, much to his surprise. Previously, they had only ever bumped elbows. Dr Venngloss said he would come the following day, and would bring Dadafarin a new mobile phone. Dadafarin waved goodbye to them, then went to his room and had a bath.

After relaxing in the bath for a while, he lay on the bed in the fluffy bathrobe provided by the hotel, and caught up on the news on television. He was heartened to see that the protest he had attended had been mostly peaceful. The party in Brixton was also described as mostly peaceful, though a small group of suspected right-wing infiltrators had apparently tried to hijack the event for unspecified nefarious reasons. According to the reporter, in spite of the violence and burning police car, the overwhelming feeling had been of solidarity and support for the BAME community. There had only been a few minor injuries.

Dadafarin had witnessed one incident mentioned on the news; the BBC reported that a policewoman had been thrown from her horse, which had been startled by the noise. Dadafarin had obviously been wrong in his observation that someone had thrown a chair at the horse, causing it to bolt beneath a traffic light and knock the police woman off. Several arrests had been made, mostly of football hooligans bent on causing chaos. Dadafarin was glad he hadn't been to a violent demonstration. Imagine the carnage.

X
DADAFARIN PREPARES FOR HIS INTERVIEW

Lesley arrived on the following Monday morning to prepare Dadafarin for his interview. Dr Venngloss hadn't turned up the day after returning him to the hotel, and Dadafarin was missing his 'phone. Unable to access the internet, he felt strangely cut off from the world. He would ask Lesley to mention it. He got dressed and made his way to breakfast, where he ate some porridge and a piece of toast before taking his coffee through to the foyer to wait for Lesley. Lesley arrived ten minutes later, dressed in a light blue suit with a mauve shirt, collar worn open with no tie. Lesley looked very elegant and smart.

Until now, Dadafarin had never seen a social justice warrior in a suit. He'd assumed that suits were symbols of the white patriarchy. After greeting Lesley, who smiled warmly as she (or he?) saw him approach, Dadafarin was invited into a small room with a plain wooden desk and three chairs, which he guessed was the hotel manager's office. Lesley began by removing "their" mask, and invited Dadafarin to do the same. 'As long as we maintain two metres distance' Lesley added, neatly folding the mask on the table. 'Let's begin, shall we?' Lesley's voice was firm yet soft, direct yet with a gentle tone. Lesley sat down and shuffled a sheaf of papers as Dadafarin took a seat on the other side of the table, then fiddled with a computer on the desk.

'I'll just be a minute' Lesley said.

Dadafarin watched as Lesley typed something into the computer. He still could not determine Lesley's gender. He wished he'd asked Dr Venngloss, but hadn't wanted to appear ignorant, or worse, bigoted. He'd sneaked a quick glance at Lesley's groin before they sat down, but that had proved inconclusive. Dadafarin decided he quite liked Lesley. In fact, he thought, if Lesley turned out to be a woman, he'd find them quite attractive. Determining Lesley's gender was made even more difficult by the fact that Dr Venngloss had referred to Lesley in the plural. Could Lesley be schizophrenic, and, to avoid stigmatization, "their" multiple personalities were acknowledged as if they were real? After all, as Dr Venngloss had said several times, an individual's truth is the only truth that matters. But surely the mentally ill, while deserving every available help and encouragement, wouldn't be allowed to practice law?

'OK, Dada, let's start' Lesley announced, looking up from "their" computer. 'The questions I am going to ask you will be very similar to the ones you will be asked in your interview. Just imagine I am an official from the Home Office. Shall we begin?'

'Yes, I am ready' Dadafarin answered. Although this was only a practice run, he felt a bit nervous.

'So, Dadafarin, what happened with your passport?' Lesley began.

'Passport? I never had a passport. I applied once, but they refused.'

'Good, excellent. And why are you seeking asylum in the United Kingdom?'

'In my country, Zoroastrians are persecuted. We are seen as infidels by the Ayatollahs, even though we follow a religion older than Islam. My whole family have disappeared, taken by the government. In Iran, until 1923, we were not allowed to ride horses, only mules or donkeys.'

Lesley looked slightly sceptical at this revelation.

'It is true. Look it up. We have always been persecuted, all through history. Under Sharia law, we only count as one fifteenth the value of a Muslim. Even Christians are not persecuted in this way, as they count as one third of a Muslim. I am the only one left free in my family, apart from my second cousin, Faridd, who I think is in Turkmenistan. But I haven't seen him for years.'

'Your whole family was arrested? Oh, gosh, how dreadful.' Lesley lost "their" composure for a moment, thin lips pursed, as if about to burst into tears. 'Do you have any proof of identity?'

'No. Is that going to be a problem?'

'It may be. But we'll get round it'

Observing Lesley while "they" asked him a few questions, Dadafarin suddenly realised the truth behind "their"plurality. Lesley suffered from nothing more than a harmless imaginary friend.

What Dadafarin had at first taken to be an involuntary twitch, where Lesley's gaze would occasionally and briefly flick to the right while talking to him, was obviously just Lesley including an imaginary friend in the conversation. Since this evidently did not affect Lesley's ability to work, everyone just acknowledged that an imaginary friend was part and parcel of what made Lesley the wonderful person they were. People in England were so inclusive. It was really moving how British people accepted others for who they were, without judgement.

Dadafarin had himself had an imaginary friend once, called Bob, whom he'd first seen in an old American western TV series. Bob was a happy go lucky kid living on a ranch in the Wild West. Bob had played with Dadafarin when the other boys didn't want to. Together, they'd hunted Indians (now of course called Native Americans) in the desert around his home. Bob had left him when he was around nine years old. He'd missed him for quite a while. Lesley's imaginary friend had obviously hung around into adulthood.

Lesley went on to ask more questions about his family, and the now-destroyed village of Mazd dal Bul, whose entire population had been forced to move to the outskirts of Tehran. So complete had been the erasure, Dadafarin said, that no trace of the village remained. It wasn't even on Google Maps any more. Most of the ancient fire temples in the region had been converted into mosques.

After a few months in Tehran, they had moved to Yazd itself, he told Lesley, where there were at least some of his people still living and the sacred fire still burned. It was in Yazd that he had been accepted into the university, only to be expelled in his second semester for not declaring his religion. Lesley listened with obvious sympathy, head cocked slightly. Dadafarin made sure to glance to his left periodically, so that Lesley's imaginary friend did not feel left out.

Next, Lesley brought out a map of Europe, and asked Dadafarin to show the route he had followed from Lampedusa, where he'd first entered the European Union. After watching him trace the route a few times, Lesley made sure he remembered it by closing the map and asking him questions about his journey. Lesley was evidently very moved by Dadafarin's story, and also extremely pleased with his preparation. After giving him a few pointers on keeping his answers concise but full of impact, Lesley brought the meeting to a close. “They” finished by asking Dadafarin how he had learnt such good English.

'When I was young, my uncle, on my father's side, visited us once from the city. He was quite rich, but he too ended up in jail. The government in Iran don't like rich Zoroastrians. Anyway, my uncle, on my father's side, he brought us a television, and set up a satellite dish on our neighbour's roof. I watched a lot of American and British television. I especially liked American westerns, because the scenery looked very much like my home area. I can still operate a lasso. In my teens, a Farsi teacher, Farside Contractor, taught me to read and write English. He was a great man. He always admired the British, as do I. He had many books, some of which were banned. I loved reading. I still do.'

'Your English is excellent' Lesley observed. 'In fact, you speak it better than some English people I know.'

'Thank you. I have been practising for many years. It is so good to be able to converse with native English speakers.' Dadafarin replied, a slight flush rising on his cheeks.

Announcing “themself” satisfied with the interview preparation, Lesley brought the meeting to a close. “They” had to go and talk to the school Ali was attending. Some students had been asking why a six-foot two boy with a long beard was attending classes. Ali was only seventeen, but was evidently an early developer. Apparently, he'd challenged a few of the boys to wrestling matches. The school needed to be more sensitive. Before leaving, Lesley handed Dadafarin a new 'phone, identical to his previous one.

'My number, along with Carey's and Dr Venngloss', are in the address book. Call me if you need anything. Good luck with your interview.'

'Thank you, Lesley. Thanks to both of you.'

Assuming he was referring to Dr Venngloss, Lesley replied, 'It's our job. And our calling. You are most welcome.'

Dadafarin walked Lesley back to "their" car, grabbed a coffee, and headed back to his room.

Back in his room, Dadafarin watched a program about climate change on the BBC. It was terrifying. Someone from a group called Extinction Rebellion presented his apocalyptic visions of the near future. Never mind 'isms, phobias or racial discrimination, apparently the whole world was about to end, consumed in an apocalyptic catastrophe of flood, fire, disease, and tempest. Mother nature was about to pay back for all those years of being trampled on by human greed.

A clip taken at the United Nations was shown, in which an angry teenager from Sweden warned her parents and everyone else's that she blamed them, and they'd better fix it, and fast. They'd stolen her innocence, her youth. Pollution was poisoning the planet, largely consisting of plastic bags and toxic fumes created by the West's addiction to burning fossil fuels. The program then became a studio debate, discussing how CO2, aircraft contrails and flatulence from cows were warming the planet at an alarming rate. There was a seemingly inexhaustible list of reasons why humans were about to become the architects of their own destruction. Apparently, everyone on the planet was going to die in the next few decades unless they gave up their cars, stopped taking holidays, and lived entirely on vegetables. Dadafarin was thoroughly shocked. It seemed the world was on an unalterable course to destruction. Feeling rather deflated, he dropped off to sleep.

XI
A VISIT FROM CAREY

The next morning, Dadafarin woke up to the insistent beeping of the telephone next to his bed. Sleepily, he picked it up and put it to his ear, but was instantly awake when he recognised the sweet voice of Carey.

'Hello? Dada?' Dadafarin's heart raced. He sat up and drew a breath, holding the 'phone against his bare chest for a moment before putting it to his ear and answering nervously.

'Hello? Carey? How are you? How wonderful to hear your voice!'

'I am good thanks! How are you?'

'Very good now, thank you.' Dadafarin apologised for sounding sleepy. Carey in turn apologised for Dadafarin missing the trip to Westfield United's football ground on the weekend.

Dadafarin had heard from Ibrahim about this outing. While he was away protesting and partying in London, the rest of the group had had a wonderful visit to Westfield United football club's stadium. They had been shown the changing rooms and Westfield United's solitary cup from their 108 years in the league, and had then been given key-rings with the team logo embellished in gold-coloured plastic. Afterwards, they had had fish and chips at the Church of Christ the Redeemer, who had organised the trip. Suitably refreshed and redeemed, they'd persuaded the bus driver to stop off at an-off licence on the way back to the hotel, where even Noureldine had bought some red wine, in a show of interfaith solidarity. Wine was, after all, symbolic of the blood of Christ, who was a prophet of Islam too.

'We know that you really missed out' Carey told Dadafarin 'but we have an even better opportunity for you. How would you like to go and stay with Grey Spinnaker?'

'Grey who?'

'Grey Spinnaker. He presents football on the television.'

Dadafarin had never heard of him. In fact, he never watched football.

'I don't know him' Dadafarin said. 'I don't know much about football.'

'Never mind. I will come round later to discuss it with you' Carey continued. 'I'll be there by 3 o'clock.'

Dadafarin was so excited at the prospect of seeing Carey that after lunch he paced around his room, continually checking the time on his 'phone, television on in the background. Ten minutes before the appointed time, he donned his smart new hoodie and made his way down to reception and sat in one of the uncomfortable armchairs in the foyer. Carey turned up ten minutes later, looking extremely beautiful in a long sleeveless dress patterned with tulips of different colours, her hair pulled back into a ponytail. They sat on one of the benches in the garden after helping themselves to coffee from the machine in the foyer. Both removed their masks, allowing Dadafarin to admire Carey's perfect teeth, beautifully framed by lips covered in bright red lipstick. How much he wanted to kiss her!

'Grey Spinnaker wants to host a refugee in his home' Carey explained. 'He is very much in favour of immigration, and has decided he wants to invite one of you to stay for a month.'

Dadafarin explained that he didn't much like football, and perhaps it would be better to invite Ibrahim, who was not only a fanatical football fan, but had even played for his local team in the Sudan. Besides which, the thought of not seeing Carey for a whole month was unbearable.

'Oh, Dadafarin, you are so thoughtful! I will ask Ibrahim then.'

Dadafarin felt elated that he had impressed Carey. She asked him if he felt prepared for his interview with the Home Office.

'Oh yes, Lesley has prepared me very well, thank you. Though I am very nervous'

Carey placed a hand on Dadafarin's leg, and his heart raced. 'You'll be fine', she reassured him 'Just don't tell them any more than they ask for'

After finishing their coffee, Carey said she had to find Ibrahim, then she had to visit another hotel. Another three boats full of migrants had arrived the day before, and she needed to make sure they were settling in OK.

XII

DADAFARIN IS INTERVIEWED BY THE HOME OFFICE

Dadafarin's interview went very well. It was conducted in the same office where Lesley had spoken to him. Two young white men, both with brown hair, black suits, black face masks and glasses conducted the interview. They almost looked like twins. They reminded Dadafarin of a film he had seen once, The Matrix. After sitting down, Dadafarin was invited to remove his mask, but, strangely, only one of the men did. Neither introduced themselves by name. The man who had removed his mask came across as sympathetic, while the other, still masked, asked more direct questions, scribbling in a notebook he had removed from his briefcase.

The two men took turns in asking him questions about Iran, why he had fled, and how he had got to the UK. His practice interview with Lesley turned out to have been perfect preparation. The masked one then asked Dadafarin what qualifications he had.

'I am a mechanic', he answered, 'A motorcycle mechanic'.

Although this was not strictly true, Dadafarin did in fact have a good working knowledge of motorcycles, especially scooters, having rebuilt several in his youth. His answer especially seemed to impress the unmasked young man, who it turned out was a motorcyclist himself.

When Dadafarin told them about his entire family being arrested, and that he still had no idea as to their whereabouts, he could tell that both men felt sympathetic. The more polite man then asked Dadafarin how he had learned such good English. They both seemed a bit taken aback that his excellent knowledge of the language had come mostly from television and books. Sensing he was losing ground, Dadafarin tried to explain further.

'My tutor, Farside Contractor, recommended many books to me. He started me with children's books, and he was such a good teacher that within a year I could read English very well. Farside Contractor had English translations of many works of Russian literature which he leant me. After we had read them we would talk about them, in English. I very much like Dostoevsky, and I love Gogol. The Overcoat is my favourite short story. We didn't have many books from Europe, but Russian literature is tolerated in Iran.'

The unmasked man looked impressed, while his colleague sat back in his chair, observing Dadafarin quietly.

'Did you go to University?' the masked man then asked, leaning forward and placing his elbows on the table. 'And which high school did you go to?'

'I was at Iranshahr High School in Yazd. I attended university in Yazd for one and half semesters, studying history. Then they removed me.'

'And why were you removed?'
'When I first registered, I did not declare my religion. I knew that someone of the Ba'hai faith had been removed from Tehran University when they discovered their religion. I decided not to lie on the form, so I left the space blank. They discovered this in my second semester, and I was expelled for withholding information.'
The man looked at his notes, then moved on to how Dadafarin had come to England. He explained his route, and made sure to stress, as Lesley instructed him, that he had not applied for asylum or been documented as a refugee in any other country. The Matrix men both seemed satisfied, and, after a few pleasantries, announced that the interview was now over.
'You'll be hearing from us in due course,' the more polite man told him, putting his mask back on.

Back in his room, Dadafarin watched a video on YouTube about police atrocities in the United States. A young girl had been shot by police a few months earlier because she tried to stab another girl with a knife. TikTok videos were shown of the young girl styling her hair, and several commentators reflected the shock many people felt that the police were now shooting children. Dadafarin had actually seen footage of this shooting on Twitter, and it had looked like the girl in the TikTok video had been just about to stab a girl in a pink jumpsuit, with the knife raised over her head when the cop shot her. However, as the American film maker Bree Newsome pointed out on Twitter, teenagers have been having fights with knives for aeons, and police shouldn't just be turning up and shooting them.

America must really be in a bad way when kids having knife fights was seen as normal behaviour, Dadafarin thought. Small wonder that people wanted change. The month before, another innocent woman had been shot when her boyfriend opened fire on police, and the police returned fire. It seemed there was no end to police violence in sight.

XIII
A DECLARATION OF LOVE

The following morning Carey arrived at the hotel just as Dadafarin was finishing breakfast. She caught his eye from reception and waved at him. He left his half-finished cup of tea, and in his excitement forgot to pick up his newspaper. In spite of the lock-down, she gave him a kiss on the cheek as he greeted her in reception, and seemed in great spirits. She had brought a book for Dadafarin to read, called White Fragility, written by Robin DiAngelo.

'Dr Venngloss said you are very interested in social justice issues' she said. 'This is currently the best book available on the subject of white privilege.'

Carey told him that the book explained all about racism, and how entrenched it was in modern society. Dadafarin had seen a few references to the book on YouTube, and it was popular on Twitter, so he was very grateful that he now had a chance to read this seminal work himself.

'How are you finding life in Britain, Dada?' Carey asked.

'Life could not be better. I am staying in a grand hotel, the weather is nice, and Britain truly is a wonderful country' he replied.

'It is all just a show' Carey replied. 'Do you have coffee in your room? We can't just stand around here' she continued.

'Yes, they have supplied a coffee making kit' he replied. 'Would you like some coffee?'

In the lift to the third floor, Dadafarin's heart was racing with excitement. He fumbled the key card before managing to open the door, and then tripped over a dirty T-shirt he had left on the floor. They both laughed, which broke some of the tension. Still flustered by the presence of Carey, Dadafarin clumsily prepared two cups of coffee, spilling a sachet of sugar all over the counter-top. Carey perched on the end of the double bed, legs crossed, watching him. She was dressed in a pink top and jeans, her hair again pulled back in a ponytail, and looked quite beautiful.

'You really are beautiful', Dadafarin said, heart pounding, as he gave her her coffee. 'I don't know how to say this, but I think I love you', he continued.

'Oh, Dada, you really are so sweet.' She stood up, cupped his face in her hands, and looked deep into his eyes. Before Dadafarin had time to think about it, he leant forward, and kissed Carey on the lips. Her lips parted, his arms slid around her back, and then they were on the bed, kissing and fumbling. Dadafarin's hand slipped under her top, and he felt a surge of excitement as he discovered she wasn't wearing a bra. Her breasts were quite small, but very firm, her body very trim. Carey pushed him away briefly, then quickly pulled her top over her head, while reaching for the clip on Dadafarin's belt, pulling him back down onto the bed.

Dadafarin was surprised how quickly events had transpired. Ever since meeting Carey, he had wondered how to make his feelings known without causing offence or embarrassment. She had previously given no indication of her attraction to him. And now, how suddenly their love was to be consummated! He was even more surprised, as his hand slid up her leg, to feel a hard protrusion. At first, he thought she had something in her pocket, but quickly realised that the protruding item was, in fact, firmly attached to her body. With a start, he jumped to his feet, looking down at Carey with an expression of shock. How could this be?

Dadafarin tried to speak, but nothing came out of his mouth. Carey covered her breasts, sat upright, and reached for her top, evidently embarrassed. She was extremely upset, tears coming to her eyes, her top lip quivering as she looked at him accusingly, as if he'd just assaulted her. Quickly putting on her top, and avoiding his eyes, she walked to the door then turned to face him, her eyes now streaming with tears, dark mascara running down her cheeks.

'Oh, Dada, I thought you were different. I thought you valued me as a human being' she said in an accusing tone as she opened the door. And with that, she was gone; he could hear her sobbing as the door closed gently on the hydraulic damper behind her, leaving him standing dazed and confused, alone in his room.

Dadafarin spent the rest of the day in bed feeling sorry for himself. The incident with Carey had been deeply disturbing. He was surprised and shocked to realise that, in spite of the very convincingly feminine Carey turning out to have a penis, he couldn't stop remembering their kiss, that feeling of bliss before his world had fallen apart. Feelings of revulsion mixed with the bitter taste of love lost battled in his confused mind, at one point reducing him to sobbing tears. After hours spent lying on the bed watching TV without really paying attention, he realised he needed to pull himself together. He had a shower and went to dinner early, glad to find that there were only two other refugees there, neither of whom he recognised.

After picking at his macaroni cheese for a while and taking an apple from the bowl on the counter, Dadafarin went back to his room and tried to take his mind off things by watching television again. It didn't work, so, remembering the twenty pounds Dr Venngloss had given him when they first met, he ventured out of the hotel grounds on his own for the first time and bought a bottle of whisky from the filling station down the road. At first he thought the man behind the counter was foreign, and had to point to the whisky behind the counter. Eventually the man managed to explain that he was from Glasgow, and could only speak English. Embarrassed, Dadafarin gave the man a tip, which seemed to confuse him greatly, and he insisted that Dadafarin took all his change. Spending the money reminded Dadafarin of the debit card Dr Venngloss had given him, onto which his benefits were paid. He still hadn't used it. Back in his room, the whisky just made him feel worse, but he eventually fell into a fitful sleep after consuming half of it. Apart from the beer he had drunk with Martin and at the street party, it was the first alcoholic beverage he had drunk since arriving in Britain.

The following morning, suffering from a hangover, Dadafarin returned to his room after a quiet breakfast and climbed back into bed with the book Carey had given him. Outside it was raining, which suited his dark mood. The outside world could go to hell, he thought to himself. He would spend the whole day reading, preparing himself for the time when he make his own way in this new world. Feeling sorry for himself was not going to help in adapting. He picked up White Fragility, sniffed the cover briefly. It still had a faint whiff of Carey's perfume on it. Sighing, Dadafarin opened the book at the place he had marked the day before with a torn-off piece of newspaper, and continued reading. It was turning out to be a very informative though somewhat confusing book.

Robin DiAngelo, in spite of being white, evidently had a good grasp of racial justice.

Dadafarin already knew that all white people were racist. Dr Venngloss had made this quite plain, and DiAngelo's book confirmed it. White people were raised to believe they were better than anyone else. Any coercion towards this view by parents or peers was unnecessary, because the entire structure of society was built around white supremacy. Merely taking your place in that society confirmed you as a racist. Denying you were a bigot merely it. This certainly tied in with all Dr Venngloss had said, but Dadafarin still found it hard to accept that the unavoidable accident of being born white sentenced you to a life of being racist.

Dr Venngloss and Carey definitely weren't racist according to any definitions Dadafarin was familiar with. Could it be possible that their dedication to Justice in Exile was in fact just a cover to hide their racism? It somehow seemed very unlikely. Even less clear was DiAngelo's statement that white men occupy the highest positions in the race and gender hierarchy. How then had Barack Obama become President? Dadafarin knew that some black men were “white adjacent”, or even “not really black”, but Obama had always struck him during his two terms as President as a very fair man. He certainly did not appear to be a racist, in spite of what the Ayatollahs claimed. After all, he'd been awarded the Nobel Peace Prize right at the start of his presidency. They wouldn't give that to a white supremacist, surely? Even a black one?

After a few hours reading, Dadafarin realised that the book was depressing him. He slept for an hour, and then went to dinner. He listened without really paying attention to a conversation

Ibrahim and Noureldine were having about some gender-neutral toilets in a supermarket they had visited. Both thought it bizarre that women were expected to use toilets where men had probably urinated on the seats. Noureldine said that non-gendered toilets basically amounted to inviting men to wave their manhood around in front of women. He asked Dadafarin what he thought about it, but getting no answer didn't press him, perhaps sensing his dark mood. After dinner, Dadafarin persuaded Claire, the receptionist, to allow him to watch a film on the hotel's pay per view for free. He watched Die Hard, which he'd already seen many times, but he felt he needed a break from social justice.

XIV
DR VENNGLOSS EXPLAINS GENDER

The next morning, Dr Venngloss arrived at the hotel just as Dadafarin was finishing breakfast, waving to Dadafarin from the door to the restaurant. Dadafarin deposited his breakfast tray, picked up his newspaper, and left the dining room. The normally cheerful doctor looked quite upset. When Dadafarin approached him, he didn't look him in the eye, and seemed rather distant.

'What is wrong, Doctor?' Dadafarin asked, although he strongly suspected it had something to do with what had transpired with Carey.

'Let's go and sit outside' Dr Venngloss replied.

They went out to the smokers alcove, sitting at opposite ends of the bench.

'Dada, I heard disturbing news about you. From Carey' Dr Venngloss announced.

'Oh yes. Carey is not really a woman' Dadafarin replied. 'But why does she look like one? I have heard this happens in Thailand, but I didn't know it happens here too.'

'Carey is a woman, Dadafarin.' This was the first time Dr Venngloss had ever used Dadafarin's full name. 'She was born with male physical characteristics, but this was not in fact her proper body for her.'

'What do you mean? Surely you are either a man or a woman?'

'No, Dada. The body you are born in does not dictate your gender. In fact, you don't have to be either a man or a woman. These are just social constructs, created by a paternalistic, patriarchal society.'

'Does this mean I am a transphobic?' Dadafarin asked. He had heard a lot about transphobia on the news recently, and on Twitter it was always being talked about. He'd never suspected Carey was in fact transgender.

'No, it means you are a misogynist.'

'Misogynist? What does that mean?' Dr Venngloss sighed, relaxing a little, his shoulders dropping. He decided to be gentle on Dadafarin. After all, he was from a completely different culture.

'Misogynist is the name given to a man who does not respect women.'

'Of course I respect women!' Dadafarin exclaimed. 'And Carey is not a woman anyway. She is a man! A man who is a transgender.'

'Carey is not transgender. She identifies as a woman.'

Dadafarin found this very confusing. He had thought he was getting to grips with identity, but it seemed he still had much to learn. 'But Carey was a man, before deciding to become a woman?' he asked Dr Venngloss.

'Carey transitioned two years ago. She was never comfortable with her birth body.'

'So she was a gay man?'

'Yes' Dr Venngloss exclaimed, exasperated. 'She

never felt comfortable with it though. I have known her since before her transition. Once she accepted that she was actually female, life became much easier for her.'
'So she was a homophobic gay man?' Dadafarin asked, evidently very confused.
'What on Earth makes you say that?'
'Well, she obviously didn't like being a gay man very much. Surely that means she was a homophobic?'
'Oh, Dada!' Dr Venngloss sighed. 'I thought you understood so much. But now I see that you still have much to learn.'
'Does this mean I should have had sex with her? Since she is a woman, and I am a straight man?'
'Well, not necessarily. But she was very upset.'
'But I don't like my women to have penises. It just doesn't seem normal.' Dadafarin was looking quite upset. 'But I do really like Carey. I was in love with her. If she didn't have a penis, I would very much like to be with her. I hope she can forgive me.'
'You have to apologise.' Dadafarin assured Dr Venngloss that he was quite happy to apologise. Secretly, he hoped that his apology would not be taken as meaning he now wanted sex with Carey, but he decided not to mention that. What a complicated world it was!

'Anyway' Dr Venngloss continued, changing the subject, 'Let's move on. How did your interview go?'
'I think it went well. I will wait and see. Lesley and

her friend prepared me very well.'
'Her friend? Was someone else with her?'
'No, only her imaginary friend. I think it's wonderfully inclusive to recognise them.'
'Dada, what on earth are you talking about?'
'Lesley has an imaginary friend. I even included her friend in our conversation' Dadafarin proudly announced.
'Lesley is non-binary' Dr Venngloss explained. 'She doesn't have an imaginary friend.'
'Non-binary? I've seen that mentioned on Twitter, and in The Sentinel, but I don't really understand it. Does it mean binary like in computer language?' Dadafarin asked, evidently confused. 'People aren't computers' he continued 'so why would you describe them in terms of computer language?'
Identity politics could be quite odd sometimes.
'Non-binary people refuse to identify as either male or female' Dr Venngloss explained. 'They are of a gender that falls outside the paternalistic hetero-normative descriptions of gender. This is why they use the pronouns they and them.'
'But Lesley is still only one person, whatever their gender. So why use plural pronouns?'

Dr Venngloss was now getting exasperated. 'Dada, it is so that people know they identify as non-binary. How else would people know?'
'Perhaps they could use the pronouns it and that?' Dadafarin suggested. 'And then people would know that they don't recognise themselves as either male or female.'

'And how would you like to be referred to as "it" or "that", Dada?' Dr Venngloss replied, putting extra emphasis on the words.

The good doctor had a point there, Dadafarin realised. He was very glad he hadn't asked Lesley to introduce their imaginary friend. It would have caused great embarrassment. Gender was just so complicated.

'Pronouns are very personal' Dr Venngloss continued. 'In fact, there are many more than just they and them. I would suggest you have a look online.'

It was so much simpler when there were just men and women, Dadafarin thought to himself. He decided to change the subject before it became any more confusing.

'I so much want to stay here in Britain. I have met so many wonderful people, and seen so many wonderful things. I am reading the book Carey gave to me, White Fragility. It must be so hard for you, being white. It seems white people are cursed with being racist. What a burden for you.'

'Indeed it is. It is a burden I will have to bear for the rest of my life' Dr Venngloss said wistfully. Dadafarin could see his eyes glazing over with shame of it. 'I blame my parents' Dr Venngloss continued. 'And not only was my father white, he was also a fascist. He voted for Margaret Thatcher. And he was also a homophobe. Once he called the local priest a dirty poof.'

'A poof? What is that?' Dadafarin enquired.

'Poof is a horrible term for gay people', the doctor

said. 'Of course, the priest deserved to be punished, because he was a paedophile and once tried to fondle me. But insulting his sexuality was a step too far.'

At this, Dadafarin's eyes lit up. 'Dr Venngloss! I have an idea! Perhaps you should be gay? That way, you would not just be an ageing white man any more. If you were gay, people would have to respect you!'

Dr Venngloss looked at Dadafarin, evidently shocked.

'I cannot pretend to be something I am not.'

'And why not? Carey is a woman because she thinks she is. You've just told me that Lesley doesn't see themselves as a man or a woman. If you decided to be a gay man, what is the difference?'

Dr Venngloss considered this for a moment, his hands folding and unfolding on his lap as he contemplated Dadafarin's words. 'I was quite attracted to a man, once', Dr Venngloss admitted wistfully. 'He was very attractive. Perhaps at the time I was homophobic, so I suppressed those thoughts.'

'You see!' Dadafarin exclaimed. 'Maybe go to a gay bar and see what happens. Noureldine tells me London is full of them, and he told me there is even one in Dorkton. Some of the guys went in there by accident. You never know. Surely it can't be worse than living as a straight white male?'

Dr Venngloss looked at Dadafarin with a new respect. He was certainly a quick learner, in spite of his terrible faux-pas with Carey. He might make a revolutionary yet.

XV
IBRAHIM RETURNS FROM HIS STAY WITH THE FOOTBALL HERO

Dadafarin spent the next ten days mostly in his hotel room. Following his conversation about pronouns with Dr Venngloss, he searched online and was shocked at the number of different identities there actually were. The list he found included seventy-eight pronouns; There was Zie, Zis, Zim, Sie, Eir,Ver, Ter, Em.... the list went on and on. How did anyone negotiate this minefield? Just They and Them had caused him enough confusion. After reading the list, Dadafarin despaired of ever coming to grips with identity. He consoled himself with the thought that at least pronouns were usually only used when referring to someone in the third person, and not to their face.

A spell of rainy weather meant walking in the gardens was not really an option, and he was still feeling quite depressed about the misunderstanding with Carey. Dr Venngloss was busy with other refugees, who were now arriving at the rate of a hundred or more every day. All needed to be housed, fed, and have their asylum claims processed. There were rumours that some of the newer arrivals were being housed in military barracks, and some of the refugees were speculating that they were all going to be locked up in concentration camps. Dadafarin knew that concentration camps had been invented by the British, and he didn't like the sound of it. Carey was not answering his calls, or his text messages.

Dadafarin found he had little in common with the other refugees, who in his opinion were largely, though by no means exclusively, fleeing poverty and uncertainty rather than terror. After finishing White Fragility, he spent some of his time reading the books that Dr Venngloss had left him. He had read the Communist Manifesto by Karl Marx and Friedrich Engels once before, but after watching a video on YouTube, he decided to read it again. In this video, one of the founders of BLM, Patrice Cullors, described herself and one of the other founders, Alicia Garcia, as trained Marxists. Being Marxist was one thing, but announcing you were trained in Marxism seemed to Dadafarin to be something else entirely. In light of this, Dadafarin found himself wondering how much Marx's thinking had informed the stated aims of BLM.

Dadafarin reread the entire book in one sitting, pausing only for lunch. Indeed, he decided after finishing the book, there seemed many parallels between social justice and Marxism; the idea of there only being two classes of people, for example. The bourgeois and proletarians had many similarities to the people of white privilege and the oppressed minorities. The idea that the family itself was a system of class oppression, the goal of rescuing education from the influence of the ruling class, these were all Marxist concepts. How could you look at images of people burning flags, and not think of Marx's statement that "The working men have no country. We cannot take from them what they have not got."

All the talk about Brexit Dadafarin had read, about white nationalists wanting to separate from Europe, all this had been neatly explained by Karl Marx and Friedrich Engels nearly 150 years ago! The dichotomy of the social justice warriors supporting gay rights while simultaneously supporting Islamic ideas, all of this could be explained by the statement that "In short, the Communists everywhere support every revolutionary movement against the existing social and political order of things." Looting was obviously acceptable when you read that "In one word, you reproach us with intending to do away with your property. Precisely so, that is just what we intend."

Dadafarin wondered why the social justice warriors rarely spoke of Communism, when it appeared that the basis of their theories largely came from the bedrock of the Communist revolution itself, the Communist Manifesto? Could it all be coincidence? Was there some form of *a priori* truth that would always resurface in times of change? Had Marx and Engels, and now the social justice movement, independently stumbled upon the answer to humanity's problems? Why then had it not worked in the Soviet Union, China, Cambodia? He wondered what Dr Venngloss would think about it all. Then he realised that the person he would most like to ask about it was Martin. But how could he find him?

Taking a break from his reading one day, Dadafarin went down to reception to get a coffee. There, unexpectedly, was Ibrahim. A few weeks earlier, Ibrahim had gone to stay with Grey Spinnaker, England football legend, now millionaire television commentator, snack salesman and campaigner for social justice. Ibrahim had told Dadafarin just before his departure that Grey Spinnaker was famous for never having been booked in his entire career.

'Hi Ibrahim. *As salamu alaikum'*

'Wa alikum asalaam, Dadafarin. How are you?'

'I am fine, thank you. How was your stay with the football legend?'

Dadafarin had only had limited conversation with Ibrahim, but had decided early on that he liked and respected him. Ibrahim seemed a very honourable man, always polite and friendly. After Dadafarin had recommended him as the refugee most deserving of this great honour, they had eaten dinner together a few times, though Ibrahim had never mentioned why he fled the Sudan.

'Let's get a coffee and sit outside' Ibrahim suggested.

It was cloudy outside, with storms threatening, but the sun was out. It was a warm day, the sound of lawn-mowers in the distance combining with the sound of birds in the trees. They sat on the grass lawn in front of the car park. A huge

storm was approaching from the west.
'So how was it?' Dadafarin asked. 'It must have been very exciting, staying with someone so famous?'
'I did not enjoy it' Ibrahim replied, frowning. 'I did not feel comfortable. Grey Spinnaker spoke to me like a child, in simple English, even putting on an accent. I never heard him speak like this with his children. Or on television.'

Ibrahim's English, though heavily accented, was as good if not better than his own. Dr Venngloss had mentioned that Ibrahim in fact had two degrees, and had worked as a teacher before he became a refugee. Dadafarin was shocked to hear about Grey Spinnaker treating Ibrahim like an illiterate. He had noticed this tendency among English people before, to talk to foreigners as if they were speaking to children, or people of low intelligence. A couple of the hotel staff spoke to them as if they were children. One of the night receptionists in the hotel, an unpleasant little fellow named Freddy, spoke like this to all the refugees, even to the extent of mimicking their accent .
'Grey Spinnaker has children?' Dadafarin enquired, sipping his coffee.
'Yes, two, a boy and a girl. They were wonderful. They asked me all about my country. If it wasn't for them, I would have asked to leave sooner.'
'You asked to leave?' Dadafarin asked, surprised.
'Yes. I was not comfortable there. He has a very large house, but it has no character. He seemed un-

comfortable around me. I felt I was there for his benefit, not mine.'
'I am truly sorry. It is my fault you went.'
'No, my brother. Sorry for what? How were you to know? It is a very strange land, this England. Everyone seems to complain all the time. They see racism where there is none, but the ones who claim to be against racism appear to hate white people. They speak of slavery hundreds of years ago, while ignoring it in the present day. I wish I could go home.'
'Perhaps one day you will' Dadafarin replied, taking Ibrahim's hands in his. 'Let's have another coffee. I'll get it. Wait here.'

Dadafarin went back to the lobby for two more cups of coffee, and took them outside. It had started raining heavily, the droplets splashing on the flagstone path which ran along the side of the hotel. Ibrahim had moved, and now sat on the smoker's bench in it's small covered alcove littered with cigarette butts. Dadafarin wondered to himself why so few people seemed to use the supplied ashtrays.
'Tell me about your journey from Sudan' Dadafarin said. 'I would very much like to hear about it.' Ibrahim sighed, his expression changing to one of sadness. After a few sips of his coffee, he told Dadafarin his story.

Ibrahim had fled South Sudan after he had been accused of consorting with Christians. A brutal attack by government troops in his village near Aweil resulted in the killing of ninety-three men, and the enslavement of eighty-five women and children. Ibrahim had been friends with several of these victims, some of whom had played in the same local football team. This connection with the Christians had resulted in him being arrested. He was awaiting trial at the Sharia court, likely to be sentenced to death as an apostate, when his uncle, a policeman, had sprung him from jail at great risk to himself.

Ibrahim's uncle had driven him to the town of Wau, concealed under a tarpaulin in the back of his pick-up. In Wau, a group opposed to the government had hidden him in a truck going to the Central African Republic. Armed with eighty US dollars and the clothes he was wearing, Ibrahim had made his way through Chad to Libya, where he had managed to get on a boat to Crete, after convincing the smugglers that his uncle was going to transfer the five thousand Euros they demanded within a few days. It was the first time in his life he remembered ever telling a lie, he told Dadafarin.

From Crete, Ibrahim had stowed away on a ferry to the mainland and then walked to Calais, foraging, begging and stealing food from fields as he went. His journey to Calais had taken him nearly two years. In the camp there, his knowledge of eight languages had enabled him to find employment as a negotiator between the smugglers and those who had the funds to make the journey to Britain. After six months thus employed, he had saved the funds necessary to make the trip himself. Though reluctant to see him go, the smugglers gave him a twenty percent discount in recognition of his contribution to their business, on condition he also recruited a suitable replacement. He had recruited a young Syrian who also spoke several languages, and had thus finally embarked on his final leg of a long and terrible journey.

After Ibrahim had told the story of his journey, silence hung over the two men for a moment, the sound of the rain now sounding insistent and loud. Dadafarin heard a peal of thunder in the distance.
'That is such a sad story' Dadafarin finally said, looking at Ibrahim. 'But now you will have a better life.' He was very moved by Ibrahim's story.
'*Inshallah*' Ibrahim replied wistfully. 'And you will too, Dada. But now tell me of your adventure in London. I heard from Noureldine that you had been arrested?'
'Yes, I had a very interesting time in London.'
Dadafarin recounted his own recent adventures, which delighted Ibrahim. Ibrahim laughed loudly at the story of Martin, tears streaming down his ebony face as Dadafarin described how Whip had ripped off his shirt and charged the police.
'I cannot remember when I last laughed like this' Ibrahim said, wiping tears from his eyes with the sleeve of his shirt 'Thank you, my brother.'

'You are most welcome. It is indeed wonderful to share our experiences.' They continued talking for some time, not noticing the cold. Later, saying goodbye in reception, they both realised that in spite of their differences, they were now firm friends.

XVI
THE EXCOMMUNICATION OF DR VENNGLOSS

A few days after Dadafarin's conversation with Ibrahim, Dr Venngloss turned up at the hotel unexpectedly. He called Dadafarin in his room, and asked if he could join him downstairs. Dadafarin was surprised to see the normally neat though cheaply dressed doctor in scruffy jeans and a shirt with a large brown stain on the front, where he had evidently spilt some coffee or tea. His face looked gaunt, he hadn't shaved for several days, and he had black bags under sunken, bloodshot eyes. The plaster on his arm had been removed, and the doctor now had the arm in a sling.

'Hello, Doctor. How are you? You do not look very well' Dadafarin greeted him. He was shocked at the doctor's appearance.

'Oh, my dear Dada, I am not well. I've not been sleeping, and I don't know who I can talk to!' Dr Venngloss replied. 'Something terrible has happened.'

'Let's get a coffee and sit in the garden' Dadafarin suggested.

The weather had improved again, and it was a warm, sunny day. Birds were calling in the forest, and a few bees were out scouting. They sat on the lawn, still damp from the recent rains, and Dr Venngloss told Dadafarin his news. He pulled out a newspaper from his man-bag, and there on the front page was a picture of Dr Venngloss with blood on his shirt, the same fascist shirt he had been wearing when they went to London. He was shaking his fist at the camera, mouth open in what Dadafarin thought was called here a snarl. Dadafarin realised that it must have been taken when they attended the BLM demonstration in London.

Dadafarin read the article, which had been penned by a journalist whose Twitter account he had recently started following, Owain Jane. Owain Jane was one of the leading lights in the social justice movement. When he had first seen Owain Jane's picture, Dadafarin had wondered how a child was allowed to have a Twitter account, much less how he managed to get a job as a journalist. The profile picture on Twitter showed what appeared to be a boy of about twelve. In fact, he was forty years old, but looked far younger. He wrote for The Sentinel, the same newspaper Dadafarin read every day, yet somehow he had missed this article. Until today, Dadafarin had thought Owain Jane a fair and unbiased man of integrity. Evidently, however, he had no scruples in getting a story.

'Read it' Dr Venngloss said. 'I am finished!'

Dadafarin took the paper from Dr Venngloss and looked at the story.

Refugee charity boss moonlights
as right-wing thug

'A white man working for a charity set up to assist refugees violently attacked peaceful BLM demonstrators at a protest in June. Dr Anton Venngloss, Chairperson of Integration and Resettlement at the charity Justice in Exile, attacked two peaceful demonstrators as they were entering Trafalgar Square. A witness who asked to remain anonymous for fear of violent reprisals told me "He was a real nutjob. He just went for them. I mean, look what he's wearing."
Shocked, Dadafarin continued reading.
'The two peaceful demonstrators managed to fight off their attacker, who had, they claimed, been approaching a man of Asian appearance with the intent of committing violence.' Dadafarin realised this was likely a reference to him. According to reliable witnesses, the article continued, the two men had approached Dr Venngloss in an effort to dissuade him. According to the article, Dr Venngloss had then attacked the two good Samaritans. "It was lucky this lunatic wasn't armed. Imagine what could have happened?" one of the witnesses said.

The article went on to speculate that Dr Venngloss was in fact affiliated with a far-right group called The Democratic Football Lads Alliance, who had been in London ostensibly to protect racist statues. Of course, this as just an excuse for attacking peaceful protestors. The fact that Dr Venngloss had admitted in a previous interview

with the paper that he was a Charlton Athletic fan, in common with well-known racist commentators like Jim Davidson, was cited as further proof of his extreme fascist leanings.
'But none of this is true! This is not possible!' Dadafarin exclaimed.
'No, of course it is not true. Evidently, the photographer who took that picture decided that as I was being confronted by demonstrators who mistook me for a fascist, that I indeed was one. Somehow, he then later identified me and sold the picture to this newspaper, who have now concocted this ridiculous story. And now, the board of trustees at Justice in Exile have seen this article. They have decided I must leave my position.'
'But surely you have explained what really happened?'
'Of course. But the trustees say that this brings the whole charity into disrepute. The charity's position is that they must avoid negative press at any cost.'

Dr Venngloss, tears in his eyes, took a sip of his coffee before continuing. 'None of my friends will talk to me any more. They have all cancelled their friendship with me on Facebook. Some have even blocked me completely.'
Dadafarin could see a stream of snot dripping from Dr Venngloss' nose. He pulled a tissue from his pocket and handed it to Dr Venngloss, who dabbed at his eyes and then blew his nose.
'Sorry, Dada, I should not be burdening you with

this.'
'No, Doctor, please. Continue. It is best to share problems.'
'I should not have been so stupid as to wear that shirt. It is all my own fault' Dr Venngloss continued. At this, the good doctor broke down and started crying.

Dadafarin was at a loss what to do. If he tried hugging Dr Venngloss, this could be construed as an unwelcome sexual advance. He had recently seen a story about this happening on the BBC. A man had been fired after putting his hand on a junior black female employee's shoulder. He had been fired for sexual assault, misogyny, and racist and patronising behaviour towards people of colour. People's feelings could be hurt so easily. It was perhaps better to only talk about feelings, rather than to act on them. Look at what had happened with Carey.
'Perhaps if I talked to your colleagues?' Dadafarin suggested.
'No, you can't do that. I would be censured for taking you to the demonstration.'
'Carey was with us. Surely she can talk to them? And your Facebook posts and Twitter account show that you are not a fascist. And how can you be forced from the charity that you created?'
'Dada, I really appreciate your concern' Dr Venngloss interrupted. 'Once this sort of thing is in the papers, there's no coming back. They will just say that my social media accounts were cover.

Nobody is going to want any association with someone who has been cancelled, just in case they are wrong in their certainty that the accused is innocent. I cannot expect Carey to speak up for someone accused of being a fascist. Some people now say I am a Trump supporter.'

Dadafarin was well aware that being called a Trump supporter was the worst insult anyone could throw at you. Trump had repeatedly been exposed as an evil, racist misogynist, especially after the infamous “grab them by the pussy” line which Dadafarin had seen quoted multiple times on Twitter. Donald Trump had grown to embody everything evil about the white imperialist hegemony that sought to control the world. In fact, the American president had a similar reputation across the globe. In Iran, he was actually considered to be an incarnation of Satan by many in the Shi'a majority.

'Though what I really don't understand' Dr Venngloss continued, 'is why anyone would think that an undercover fascist would get involved in a violent public demonstration, and pointlessly destroy his cover?'

Dadafarin was at a loss for words. How could the people fighting for a free society turn so suddenly on one of their own? How could the media claim to be fair? Was The Sentinel actually any better than the people it vilified? Perhaps the liberal press was still infected with the lingering after-taste of systemic colonial hypocrisy, without even realising it. After all, Owain Jane was himself a white man. According to Robin DiAngelo and the tenets of social justice, he was therefore a racist himself. The problem wasn't systemic racism or systemic patriarchy, the problem was the system itself, the entire structure of society. That's why the anarchists and antifascists wanted to break everything, Dadafarin realised. It could not be fixed, as Marx himself had said. Everything was corrupt, even the opposition.

'What will you do?' Dadafarin asked.

'I don't know. I really don't know.'

Dadafarin didn't know what else to say. Here was a man who had dedicated his life to helping those less fortunate than himself, assisting those fleeing tyranny in finding a new life, in a new country. And now, the ideology he believed in so much had turned against him, all because he'd worn the wrong shirt one day. It just showed how aware you needed to be about the evils of patriarchal white supremacy. Even your choice of clothing could ruin your life.

XVII
DADAFARIN SELF-ISOLATES

The day after receiving the terrible news of Dr Vengloss' excomummuinication, more bad news was announced at breakfast by the Assistant Human Resources Manager, a young woman named Kelly. Apparently two of the hotel guests had been diagnosed with Covid 19. As a result, from that evening everyone would be confined to their rooms. Food would be delivered to their rooms, and they were only allowed out once a day for exercise, on their own, in the hotel grounds. As compensation, they were to be given free movies on the hotels pay per view channel. Back in his room, Dadafarin found himself getting a bit depressed about the idea of of ten days confined to his room. After watching a few movies, he soon lost interest.

Dr Venngloss was now banned from the hotel, since he no longer had a reason to be there, and Carey hated him. The television soon got boring, and the BBC seemed to only report on the government and Covid restrictions. Every day the Prime Minister or one of his cabinet would deliver a Covid briefing, but these soon became very repetitive. Dadafarin found himself spending more and more time on Twitter. He had created a new Twitter account on his replacement 'phone, not knowing how to log back in to his original account after losing his original 'phone in London. It took a while to find everyone he had been following, but he soon got his new account up and running.

Dadafarin was now following a selection of celebrities, journalists, political commentators, and a surprising amount of white people who weren't happy with their skin colour. After posting replies to a few tweets, he was excited one day to gain his first follower, apart, of course, from Dr Venngloss, though the doctor had fallen silent on Twitter since losing his job. Many people on Twitter had evidently been delighted by the good doctor's fall from grace, and Dadafarin had even seen a few very nasty memes about it.

Twitter was like another world. On Twitter, people really seemed to connect with their inner anger. They didn't didn't stop at saying they didn't agree with someone, they wished death, plague or even a horrible death on them. It was the front line of the ongoing battle in identity politics, where society's new ideas were bandied about. People were continually being called out for being 'ists or 'phobes, and the wrong word could see you banned. If you repeated anything at all that Donald Trump had said, you could be immediately banned. Twitter moderators acted as the morality police, removing tweets and banning people whose comments went too far to the right.

Dadafarin realised he needed to update his idea on what constituted right wing politics. Right wing actually seemed to mean anyone who didn't agree with the social justice warriors. Rather than just being a political leaning, right wing was actually evil, encompassing every vice known to man, although it seemed that men dressing up in women's clothes and declaring that they were actually female received some sort of exemption. At least Carey looked like a woman; on Twitter men with beards were complaining about not being allowed in women's toilets. Dadafarin was also very surprised that some of the loudest and most aggressive voices on Twitter were the ones promoting fairness and equality the most. It seemed that if you were really deeply committed to equality, you needed to get very angry. Shouting was done by using capital letters. Dadafarin had however been pleasantly surprised by how so many Hollywood celebrities, musicians and successful sportsmen were taking time out from their busy lives to tell the public how unfair, bigoted and discriminatory life was for those less fortunate than themselves. Who better for highlighting inequality than a rich celebrity living in a ten-bedroom house?

Britain's own Prince Harry, after marrying his American wife, had very quickly joined the ranks of the social justice warriors. Now, he was speaking out about injustice, poverty, racism and privilege, in spite of the couple's calls for respecting their privacy. His American wife, in spite of her Mediterranean appearance and light skin, had herself been subject to racist attacks in the media.

Race seemed an extremely complex and nuanced subject. Apparently, even calling a black person a hypocrite was racist, because no white person could have any idea of that person's lived experience. Qualifying as black was seemingly dictated by having even the smallest amount of genetic material inherited from someone of African origin, although evidently there was also a requirement that you supported BLM, transgender people, and Islam. Although men could identify as women, and women as men, white people could not identify as black. It was also a requirement of being black that you didn't vote for Donald Trump, as the Democratic nominee for President, Joe Biden, had made very clear recently when he said that any black people voting for Trump "ain't black".

Actors in particular seemed to be very socially aware. Although they were themselves less likely to be victims of white supremacy, the only real danger in their life being the casting couch, they were acutely aware of the disparities in living conditions between themselves and people less fortunate. Their outspoken support for oppressed minorities proved that their comfortable living standards didn't mean that they couldn't empathise with those who daily faced the risk being shot by the police, or of being refused a job or university place based on racist ideas such as merit.

In America, and seemingly in the United

Kingdom too, systemic racism was so endemic that it was now deemed necessary to introduce racial bias training. To make this fair, white people and people of colour attended different courses in many establishments. The University of Kentucky had decided that the best way to ensure equality among its teaching staff was by segregating the anti-racism training given to incoming resident assistants; in separate classes, the white applicants were required to acknowledge their racial guilt, while the BIPOC applicants were given sympathy and understanding, amid heartfelt assurances that the University would do all in its power to protect them from the insidious racism prevailing throughout the country. Several academics had been dismissed for questioning this approach. You could obviously not create fair discourse without first removing dissent.

The New York Times had taken social justice to new levels, re-examining history to fit the new narrative. Dadafarin was surprised to find that they had initiated something called the 1619 project, which was currently one of the top trending hashtags on Twitter. The premise of this initiative was that America had not actually been founded with the Declaration of Independence at all. This document, on which the whole political structure of the United States was founded, was in reality just an attempt to maintain slavery. America had in fact been *founded* on slavery in 1619, when the first slaves had been sold on mainland

North America. Dadafarin found this fascinating, as he had always been under the impression that the Spanish had brought slaves to the Americas from Africa much earlier than this. He decided to check.

A quick search on Google told Dadafarin that in fact the first *official* slave in what would become the United States was owned by Anthony Johnson, himself a black man and a former indentured worker. In 1654, an indentured servant in his employ, John Casor, reached the end of his indenture period, and left to work for another landowner. Anthony Johnson took the case to court and won, and John Casor was declared Mr Johnson's property, effectively making John Casor the first officially sanctioned slave in what was to become the United States. The fate of the four white indentured servants also in Mr Johnson's employ remains unknown. Dadafarin was surprised in light of this discovery that the 1619 project was not instead called the 1654 Project. Although, as one commentator on Twitter pointed out, indentured servitude was tantamount to slavery anyway, with the only difference being it wasn't necessarily a life sentence.

By the end of the first week of isolation, Dadafarin was getting bored. He'd read a few of the books given to him by Dr Vengloss, but the only one he really enjoyed was All Quiet on the Western Front, by Erich Maria Remarque. Dr Vengloss had told him that the book had been banned by the Nazis, for fear of it putting young Germans off the idea of war. All Quiet on the Western Front told the gripping and terrible story of a German soldier's experiences on the Western Front in World War One, and was a truly disturbing read. After finishing it, Dadafarin couldn't help feeling that perhaps some of the complaints of people nowadays seemed a bit trivial compared to the prospect of being eaten alive in a muddy trench by rats while having high explosives and gas chucked at you constantly, your only hope of a break in routine being to run across thick churned up mud while people fired at you with machine guns. Lockdown or the threat of being offended by someone's choice of words did not seem quite so bad in comparison.

XVIII
AN OUTING

Finally, the two-week self-isolation imposed on the refugees ended. To make up for their incarceration, the Church of Christ the Redeemer had arranged a day out. They were to visit Chartwell House, which had been the home of Winston Churchill, the wartime Prime Minister who had saved Britain from the Nazis, but who was now considered to have been an extreme fascist himself judging by some articles in the media. Dadafarin was really excited about the visit. As a boy he had studied the Second World War, and found it a fascinating period of history. Farside Contractor had among his extensive library several books about this worldwide conflict.

Iran itself had played a part in World War II, though not as a combatant.

In revolutionary Iran, the invasion of the country by the Allied Powers in 1941 was held as incontrovertible proof that the United Kingdom was obsessed with conquering foreign countries and stealing their resources. At this uncertain stage of the war, a neutral Iran was of serious concern to Britain and the USSR. They wished to safeguard supplies from the Abadan oil refinery, and also to ensure that the Trans-Iranian Railway could be used by the Americans to supply the Soviet Union, under the lend-lease arrangements put in place after the invasion of the USSR by the Nazis in June 1941. The strategic importance of these, and the Allied worry that Axis forces were planning their own invasion, caused Allied forces much concern.

After pressure was put on Reza Shah, the ruler of Iran, to expel German nationals from the country, anti-British protests had erupted. This was conveniently seen by Britain as showing pro-German sympathies, and in late August the invasion began. The British invaded by sea from the Persian Gulf, and the Russians by land from the north. The Iranian forces were no match for the British and Russian forces, and the invasion was over in six days. Reza Shah abdicated, and his son Mohammed Reza Pahlavi became ruler, a position he held until the Islamic Revolution of 1979, ending 2500 years of continuous Persian monarchy dating back to Cyrus the Great.

After breakfast, a large bus pulled up in front of the hotel. Dadafarin was surprised to see many new faces. Evidently the lifeline for refugees across the English Channel was still very active. He found Ibrahim talking to another man of Sudanese appearance, and they invited him to sit with them on the bus. A holiday atmosphere livened proceedings as the throng waited to board the coach. Noureldine even said hello. When the bus doors opened, the waiting crowd pushed and jostled to get on board, until a young man, one of the volunteers from the church, shouted at them to form a line. Entering the bus, they were given small bottles of water and were told that they must keep their masks on. Dadafarin and his companions found seats near the back of the bus. Ibrahim sat on one side of the aisle with his friend, and Dadafarin sat on the other next to Noureldine, who grunted as Dadafarin sat next to him. It was going to make drinking the water difficult.

When the bus was under way, Noureldine grunted again. Dadafarin couldn't make out what he was saying through the mask. Noureldine then pulled off his mask, grimacing.

'These masks. You cannot breathe. Or talk.'

'Yes, they do make it difficult', Dadafarin replied. 'But it is all for the best. For the public health.'

'I am not so sure' Noureldine replied. The young man who had told them to form a line then noticed that Noureldine wasn't wearing his mask, and shouted at him from the front of the bus to put it on. Cursing, Noureldine replaced his mask.

'Where are you from?' Dadafarin asked Noureldine. Although they had both arrived together, they had rarely spoken. Dadafarin was suspicious of Noureldine. He looked Arabic in appearance, though had quite dark skin. He was short and stocky, with short black hair, a face that had evidently been ravaged by acne at some point, and had a thin scar on his left cheek which looked like it had been put there with a sharp blade. He looked the type of person that, if you encountered them on the street, your initial instinct would be to cross

the road.
'I am from Syria. But you know that already. I had to flee my country, like you. But you were not on the boat with us? How did you arrive?'
'I was on a different boat' Dadafarin replied. 'There were only four of us. It was a very small boat, like a children's toy.'
'What happened to the other three who travelled with you?' Noureldine enquired, his strangely deep brown yet piercing eyes looking at Dadafarin.
'They ran away as soon as we landed.'
'But we never saw another boat?' Noureldine continued.

Dadafarin didn't like where this line of insistent questioning was going. Did Noureldine somehow think he was making it all up? This was truly bizarre.
'The boat got washed back out to sea. Did you not see the coastguard boat picking it up? I wanted to claim asylum, but my companions wanted to go to London and find work. When I saw your boat, and saw the police arrive, I knew that they were going to arrest you. So I joined you. It was easier than explaining exactly what had happened. But why, what's the problem?'
'Nothing, my friend' Noureldine said, and offered his hand. Aware of social protocols, Dadafarin instead bumped elbows. On the way to Chartwell House, after some prompting from Dadafarin, Noureldine told his story.

'I was born in Al Bab, in the north of the country. My family were cannabis sellers. Hashish and marijuana. Very successful, too. My father and my grandfather before him were famous throughout the region. We imported hashish from Lebanon and Pakistan, cannabis from Turkey and Jordan. My grandfather even sold majoun from Egypt for many years. Majoun is made from honey, almonds and hashish. Sometimes it has opium in it. It is a traditional delicacy, much favoured by older people, and it is still used in some parts of Morocco. It is very nice.' Noureldine smiled, the first time Dadafarin had seen anything except a scowl on the young man's face.
'My father moved us to Al-Raqqah, then the war came. The city was at this time controlled by the militias. My father got tired of paying *baksheesh*, so one day, instead of paying the local militia chief, who was aligned with Assad, he greeted him with a shotgun. By this point, the civil war was everywhere. This was before the Russians came.'

'Assad had never been popular in Al-Raqqah, and it looked as if he was going to be defeated. My father thought that this militia chief would be too scared to do anything. What could he do? Most of the area was already under the control of the YPG. But this man was very clever. He did not tell his colleagues that this was about *baksheesh.* No, he told them that my father, and all of his family, were members of ISIL. This was when

ISIL still controlled much of the area around Al-Raqqah. The front line was only a few miles away. The whole area was being destroyed. So my family fled. They decided to join the YPG in fighting ISIL. I did not go with them.'

'Why did you not go with your family?' Dadafarin enquired after he realised Noureldine had finished his story.

'I have no interest in fighting. What for? Democracy? What is democracy? Just so another crazy person can run things for his own benefit? Or for religion? I am not religious.'

'But you give the appearance of being a Muslim? You don't eat pork, and you don't seem to like the church much' Dadafarin observed.

'It is better to be seen as religious if you want asylum, I have been told. I am a Turkman. My people were originally from Turkey, but a long time ago. But my family has never followed religion much. The imam's don't much like our kind. Though my uncle is an imam.'

'So you are not here because of persecution?'

'Shhh' Noureldine said. 'Yes, I am. And please, never speak of this talk. I should not have told you. You will not mention it to Dr Venngloss?'

'Of course not. I will not mention it to anyone. But why did you tell me this? How do you know you can trust me?'

'In my work, it is very necessary to be able to tell if you can trust people. By, what do they call it, in-

stinct? I know you are a good man. I have seen you.' Noureldine tapped his nose. 'But, if you tell anyone, you also know I will kill you.'
This shocked Dadafarin. 'Kill me?'
'No, don't worry. Just joking. Because I know I can trust you.' Noureldine tapped his nose again, a gesture that Dadafarin did not know how to interpret.

They were interrupted by the young man standing up at the front of the bus. He tapped a microphone in his hand, nearly deafening everyone. He fiddled with a switch on the microphone, which then emitted a loud screech of feedback. The driver took the microphone from him and switched it off.
The young man shouted out 'Can you hear me?' Once he was satisfied everyone was listening, he told them that they would be there for two hours, and the guide showing them around would give a commentary in English. Those who understood English were encouraged to help with translating the commentary for those who could not. They were honoured to be the first people to listen to the National Trust's brand new presentation about the history of Chartwell House, and it's most famous resident, Winston Churchill. With a buzz of excitement, the men alighted from the bus into a light drizzle, where their guide was waiting for them on the gravel drive under a large golfing umbrella.

XIX
THE IMPERIALIST HOUSE OF A BRITISH HERO

The house of Winston Churchill was a large red brick house set in parkland. Dadafarin was slightly disappointed, as he'd been expecting a palace. The rain suddenly became heavier, so they were ushered through the door into a large hall by the young lady with an umbrella. She was dressed in a short skirt and a white blouse, and looked to be in her early twenties.

'Welcome!' she greeted them, having shaken her umbrella at the door and placing it in a stand. 'My name is Maisie, and I'll be your guide today! Please wipe your shoes!'

Maisie seemed very cheerful. They were told to keep their masks on, maintain social distancing as much as possible, and instructed to use the hand sanitisers regularly. Unfortunately, Maisie informed them, much of the house was actually closed due to the ongoing program of decolonising the exhibits.

The estate on which Chartwell stood dated back to 1382, Maisie announced, and was in those days called Well-street, owned by a William-at-Well. Later it was owned by a Potter family for several centuries. They passed an open door into a large sitting room, with an orange couch and two large armchairs. 'That is one of the drawing rooms'

Maisie explained, though Dadafarin could not see any evidence of the artistic pursuits he knew Churchill had enjoyed. 'But we will start with the library.' Her talk on the history of the house turned to Winston Churchill, it's most famous occupant. 'Churchill plotted many of his colonial exploits in this very room' they were told, looking into the library with it's well-stocked shelves. 'It is probably in this room that he planned the Bengal Famine' she continued.

They continued on to Churchill's studio, where he had painted his paintings and written some of his books. Maisie went on to tell them of Churchill's early life as a war correspondent in the Boer war, his service in the Sudan, and how in the First World War he oversaw the disastrous campaign at Gallipoli.

Much to Dadafarin's surprise, Maisie then went on to explain a recently updated and revised history of Churchill regarding World War II. Never mind that he did in fact save Britain from the Nazi menace: in light of the calls for fairness, equality and a less blinkered interpretation of Britain's past, the Trust felt duty bound to present the real history behind his manic reign during World War Two. Soggy cigar clenched in his portly mouth, his real mission had been the continuation of the British Empire. Churchill had exhorted the head of Bomber Command, Bomber Harris, a power-mad despot, to completely obliterate the people of Germany. They then set about a systematic genocide of German civilians, reigning terror from the sky on German cities in an indiscriminate bombing campaign that continued until the wars end.

Dadafarin had recently watched an old BBC documentary about Churchill, which portrayed him as the greatest Briton ever. Far from portraying him as the hero who had saved Britain in its darkest hour, however, here he was being portrayed by Maisie, in his own house, as a psychotic lunatic. When Maisie went on to describe the Bengal Famine of 1943 as a deliberate attempt to starve the population, Dadafarin realised that perhaps she had been influenced by current trends. There seemed to be large gaps in her understanding of what World War II was all about. Very little of Maisie's commentary centred on the fact that Britain had been the last bastion against Nazism in Europe before Hitler's invasion of Russia. There was no mention of Dunkirk, the Battle of Britain or D-Day.

Churchill's famous, rousing speech delivered after the Battle of Britain was never even mentioned, although Noureldine told Dadafarin later that this speech had in fact been showing on a small television in a very dark room with no heating. Dadafarin found himself wondering how history could be so different, depending on how you viewed it. He wished he could chat with Dr Venngloss about it, and felt a twinge of sadness as he wondered if he would ever see the good doctor again.

Dadafarin left the group, no longer interested in the tour. Outside, it had stopped raining, so he found a bench in the gardens and sat down, taking off his mask. Ibrahim had followed him outside, and joined him on the bench.

'Are the British no longer proud of Churchill?' Ibrahim pondered, offering Dadafarin a piece of chewing gum.

'Perhaps they are not' Dadafarin replied. 'It seems to me that a lot of British are ashamed of their own history. Of course, every country has some bad history. But you cannot change it.'

'I think they don't really know what bad is any more' Ibrahim replied looking down at his hands, clasped loosely on his knees. 'It's funny that to us, this country means freedom, yet to the English it seems it is never going to be free enough. I wonder if they have lost their perspective? They are more free than perhaps any other people in the world, yet many of them seem to imagine they are oppressed. I sometimes wonder if the reason they welcome refugees is that they envy the repression we have suffered. Their lives are soft, and they have lost the balance by which to judge.'

'Yes, perhaps that is it' answered Dadafarin. 'There is much I don't understand about them. But if we wish to make this our home, it is better we accept their ways.'

Maisie appeared from a side-door of the house, tutted loudly, and took a few steps along the gravel path towards them. Her heels sank into the gravel, making her walk like a drunk. 'We've been looking everywhere for you.' Maisie announced, sounding exasperated. 'The tour is over, and everyone else is already back on the bus.' She then curtly spun round, twisting her leg as again her shoe sank into the gravel, and marched off unsteadily around the corner of the house,.

The sound of the gravel crunching under her shoes for some reason reminded Dadafarin of the sound of marching soldiers. The two friends made their way back to the bus, taking the same seats they had occupied on the way there. Neither were surprised to find that everyone else seemed to share the peculiar feeling of melancholy the tour of the house had given them. The return journey was much quieter, and Dadafarin slept most of the way.

XX
FINDING MARTIN

Dadafarin was starting to get bored with life in the hotel, though there were a few interesting developments, not least being Noureldine's new though unpaid job assisting in the kitchen. Food always seemed a constant topic of debate among the refugees. Early in Dadafarin's stay, there had been some concern about whether the meat was halal, forcing the hotel to change their supplier. Several of the residents then took to complaining loudly about the menu. Even Dadafarin, generally not fussy about his food, had found that the menu was by now getting repetitive, with the chefs struggling to think of dishes that wouldn't offend anyone.

Things came to a head after lunch one day when Amir, a refugee from Pakistan, mentioned to Ardy Shah, Dr Venngloss's replacement, that they were often served Indian dishes, yet there wasn't a single Indian refugee in the hotel. Mr Shah had taken this very seriously, and the same evening at dinner had brought the kitchen staff out of the kitchen to answer the refugee's complaints. The chef, Thomas, evidently annoyed at his culinary skills being challenged, pointed out that being British, in Britain, meant that he cooked mainly British food. The refugees were in fact very lucky, Thomas continued, that curry had been the *de facto* national dish of Great Britain since the 1970's. Chicken tikka masala had been invented in a restaurant in Glasgow, Scotland. No one had yet complained about his lasagne, Thomas pointed out, and none of the refugees were Italian. At that he had turned on his heel and stormed back to the kitchen. He was never seen again.

Shortly after the disappearance of Thomas, while collecting his newspaper one morning Dadafarin asked Claire what had become of the chef. In conspirational tones, Claire told him that for his cultural insensitivity, Thomas had been ordered to attend a Diversity, Equity and Inclusivity training session. Dadafarin had in fact also overheard two of the restaurant staff talking about it in breakfast one morning: at the time, Dadafarin had wished Dr Venngloss was still around, so that he might ask if could attend the course too.

Claire explained that Thomas' training did not go well. The insensitive chef had apparently accused the Human Resources staff running the course of being guilty of patronising minorities, by telling white people how to interact with them. They were thus exhibiting racism themselves. For this gross insult, Thomas was fired. Phil, his young assistant, was promoted to head chef. On hearing of Thomas' departure, Noureldine offered to help in the kitchen, and his request was granted. The food improved dramatically.

In addition to the improvement in the menu, lock-down had been relaxed, and people

were now allowed to gather in groups of six. It made little difference to Dadafarin, as he only knew four people he would like to spend time with, and one of those would never talk to him again. Another had vanished; Dr Venngloss's mobile phone seemed to have been disconnected. Dadafarin really missed his talks with Dr Venngloss. He also kept thinking of Martin, and he had been given an idea about finding him while talking to one of the security guards one day. Dadafarin mentioned to Igor that Martin had been busking when he met him.
'If he's a busker, where you saw him is probably his pitch' Igor told him. Igor went on to explain that buskers jealously guarded their 'pitch', the place where they performed. In a busy place like Marble Arch, which was where Igor thought Dadafarin had probably met Martin, a busker would only have access to the pitch at certain times. So, to find Martin, all Dadafarin had to do was go there at the same time of day he had met him, preferably on the same day of the week. Dadafarin immediately decided to go the very next Saturday, and Igor announced that he would be on a day off. He said he would like a trip to London, and would act as Dadafarin's guide if he so wished.

Dadafarin wasn't really sure why he wanted to see Martin again. He thought it was probably because, of everyone he had met so far, Martin seemed the least bound by worries of how he appeared to anyone else. He had given Dadafarin the impression of being an observer, rather than a participant, in spite of his enthusiastic embrace of rioting as entertainment. Every other English person Dadafarin had met, though admittedly that wasn't very many, seemed to always talk through a sort of filter, carefully replacing any words that could be construed as old-fashioned or bigoted. Some spoke to him in the way Ibrahim had described Grey Spinnaker talking, as if they were talking to a child.

Dadafarin had found that a lot of people in England seemed extremely self-conscious, judging from the media and his limited experience of the general public. Although people often spoke to him as if scared of upsetting him, they also seemed overly concerned with impressing each other. Whip, for example, had obviously been very taken with his own image as a revolutionary. He didn't appear to be doing things for himself, but for how it looked to other people. Sitting topless on that piano, he had been acutely aware of how he looked. Just before they had left to go to the party, before putting on more clothes, he had asked Kyla to take several pictures with his 'phone before they set off to the party. He had then posted them on Instagram, proudly showing Dadafarin his picture and how many followers he had. Whip had also taken selfies of himself several times on their journey, including on the tube train. At the party, Dadafarin had even seen a masked Antifa soldier pick up a brick and hold it at arms length, taking a selfie with his other hand before launching the brick at the police. At the demonstration, it had seemed that is was more important for many of the demonstrators to take selfies than take part in the demonstration.

Many of the refugees also had this strange Western selfie affliction, but they hadn't learned it here: like most trends in Western culture, it had soon found it's way around the world. Dadafarin passed them almost daily, phone at arm's length, posing for selfies, smiling manically at the camera in front of a pot plant, their lunch or a road sign, sometimes in groups. Dadafarin doubted Martin really cared about his image; he was just a participating observer, in what someone had once said was 'life's rich tapestry'. And now, hopefully, he was going to find out if he was right.

Igor picked Dadafarin up in his car at eleven o'clock on the Saturday morning. They had worked out that Dadafarin must have met Martin at around five o'clock in the afternoon. They were going to leave Igor's car at his cousin's house in Lewisham. They would then catch something called a DLR, then a tube train, to Marble Arch. On the way they would drink some beers, as since Super Saturday the bars were now open, under strict rules. Dadafarin wondered how they were going to drink beer while wearing masks. After dropping Igor's car, a short walk took them to the DLR, which turned out to be a train.

After a short wait, a silent train pulled up

and they took seats at one end of a mostly empty carriage. A group of women in chadors sitting at the opposite end of the carriage brought back a childhood memory. Dadafarin remembered once as a child, on another train, watching a group of dark-clothed women wearing chadors, their hands disappearing behind their veils to place food in their mouths, their hands making the veils twitch, like a strange puppet show.

'Where are you from, Dadafarin?' Igor asked, snapping him out of his daydream.

'I am from Iran.' He explained to Igor how he had come to be in Britain.

'And you, Igor? Where are you from, and what brings you to Great Britain?'

'I am from Romania. My wife is from here. I miss my country, but I get paid more here. One day I will go home.' Igor told Dadafarin about his two children, Andrei and Elena, and his wife Christina, who was a nurse. He'd been in Britain for twelve years, but owned a small farm in Romania, which his brother ran for him. They planned on retiring there.

The twenty five minute train ride passed quickly, as Igor told Dadafarin about Vlad the Impaler, the inspiration for Dracula. Vlad had been born in the same town as Igor. Igor's enthusiasm for the gruesome story was slightly disturbing, and Dadafarin found himself hoping that the huge Romanian was not too much of a fan of bloodshed. Don't be stupid, Dadafarin told himself. Igor seemed to be a very nice man.

Leaving the DLR at Bank, a short walk brought them to the tube station, then a short ride through the bowels of London on a noisy and rickety train full of drunk people. They arrived at Marble Arch around 3pm, and wandered off into the back streets until they found a bar, a colourful sign outside showing that it was named The Rainbow Unicorn. Inside, it looked very much like the traditional English bars Dadafarin had seen on television and in films. The bar wasn't very busy. A group of young women at one table were all looking at their 'phones. A young lady led them to a table and told them a waiter would be with them shortly. They removed their masks, and immediately an effeminate Italian-looking man in a Lycra T-shirt appeared.

'You can only take your masks off when you are sitting down' the young man announced.

Wha' can I get ya?' the waiter enquired, pulling a pencil from behind his ear and whipping a notepad from a pocket tied to his waist, all in one fluid motion. Dadafarin wondered if he had practised this move in front of a mirror. Igor ordered two pints of Old Speckled Hen, which somehow didn't sound very appetising. When the waiter returned with their beer, Igor asked him how old the bar was, and how it had got such an unusual name.

'Ah, I dunt naa how old it is' the young man replied. 'But I fink it's very old.' He then went on to tell them the pub had been renamed recently. Some people had found its original name, The Black Rose offensive. The owner of the pub didn't agree with this sentiment, moaning about 'goddamn snowflakes.' However, he had caved in to commercial pressure; his pub had only just been able to open again after months of no trade due to the virus.

The landlord had chosen the new name as he felt it aligned with the sentiments of the protestors who had been so offended by it being called the Black Rose. After several beers, which tasted as horrible as it's name, they left the pub and walked back towards Marble Arch. Approaching the tube station, they could hear the sound of a trumpet. Dadafarin felt a surge of excitement, pushing past two elderly people dressed as punk rockers who were arguing on the pavement as he rushed towards the station. To his delight, as he got nearer he could see that yes indeed, it was Martin!

XXI
FRIENDS REUNITED

Martin was playing a jazz song as they approached him. At least, Dadafarin assumed it was jazz, because whatever he was playing, it did not seem to have any structure. Martin was dressed in multi-coloured trousers, wearing a dark and well-worn shirt that said Free Palestine in faded letters across the front. When Martin noticed Dadafarin, he smiled and winked, and carried on playing his trumpet, but with a renewed vigour now. It was quite busy around the tube station, and people dropped coins in the top hat Martin had placed on the pavement as they rushed to catch the tube. Martin finished his song with a last flourish, pointing the trumpet at the sky as he did so, and then placed the trumpet in its case before greeting Dadafarin.

'Dada! What a surprise! How are you?' Martin gave Dadafarin an exaggerated elbow bump, the standard form of greeting now in these times of plague, and looked quizzically at the huge bulk of Igor standing next to Dadafarin.

'I am good, thanks! This is Igor' Martin bumped elbows with Igor, and then asked Dadafarin what brought him to London.

'I came to find you, Martin. I enjoyed our time together, and thought it would be nice to see you again.'

Igor suggested they go back to the Rainbow Unicorn for refreshments, and to celebrate the reunion. Back in the pub, the same socially-distanced table Igor and Dadafarin had sat at previously was still available. The same group of young women were still there, evidently quite drunk now judging by the increase in volume since Igor and Dadafarin had left the pub. One of these young women was gurning at her 'phone, lips pouted as she took several selfies. Igor ordered three pints of Old Speckled Hen from a young female waiter.

'Can I just have lager?' Dadafarin asked. He hadn't enjoyed the Old Speckled Hen, which tasted as bad as it sounded. Shortly, the waiter returned with their beers. The lager tasted much better.

'So Martin, how is the revolution going?' Dadafarin asked, at which Igor raised his eyebrows before gulping down half of his pint of beer in one go.

'Ah, the revolution. The revolution is not really happening. I am no longer with Antifa.'

'No? What happened?' Dadafarin asked.

'Well, it was fun for a while. But after I became a full black bloc member, I realised that it's more about destroying things than building them.'

'Black block? What is that?'

'Black bloc is the military arm of Antifa You see them dressed completely in black at demonstrations. Their job is to stir up the crowd into violent action. They smash shop windows to encourage the crowd to start looting, build barricades, and whip up the crowd. They also harass people, and dox them.'

'Dox? What's that?' Igor interjected. 'Do they give them diseases?'

'Not pox' Martin replied, laughing. 'Dox. Doxxing is where you publish someone's address online, or make known their current whereabouts' he explained. 'Then people can harass them. Not necessarily violently. I was once sent round to a journalist's house with two other guys just to stare at him. We rang the doorbell and just stared at the guy when he answered. It's very effective.'

'It sounds terrible' Igor said. 'You should be ashamed of yourself.'

'Well, yes, it was that incident that was the last straw for me. I thought I was involved in bringing about social change. Then I realised that Antifa are not interested in change, beyond the process of actually instigating it. They don't appear to have a plan beyond bringing down capitalist society. I decided that being a socialist does not have to involve violence. Not if you really care about people. Since I left, I have been subjected to doxxing myself, to make sure I don't publicise anything about the group I was with. Now I'm just an anarchist.'

'That sounds terrible' Igor repeated. 'Let's order more beer.'

Dadafarin asked Martin why BLM didn't stop Antifa groups from attending their demonstrations. 'Surely they know what Antifa's real objectives are?'

'Of course they do. I was at a meeting where we were discussing tactics with them. We provided security for their marches.'

Dadafarin was very surprised by this. As far as he knew, BLM were only interested in racial equality. He couldn't help wondering if Martin was exaggerating.

'So why did you get involved at all?' Igor asked, draining his second pint and signalling the waiter to bring more.

'Well, it seemed a good idea at the time' Martin replied. 'Social justice, sticking up for the underdog, fighting fascism. But in reality, Antifa are more fascist than the people they claim to be fighting. It's a crock of shit. The whole world is a crock of shit.'

After Martin had explained to both of them what a crock of shit was, an uneasy silence settled around the table. Dadafarin became aware of raised voices behind him. At the other end of the bar, they heard glass breaking, and turned round to see a young woman in a tight faux leather miniskirt, halter top and heels staggering backwards clutching her face, screaming. Blood appeared through her fingers, and she sank to the floor. She appeared to have just had a glass smashed in her face. A thick-set bouncer in a cheap looking suit rushed towards another woman, dressed almost identically to the other, but several sizes larger. The bouncer grabbed her by the shoulders, and then forced her arms behind her back. He started pushing her towards the door as she screamed and yelled, the woman who had been hit by the glass watching from her position sprawled against a radiator below the window. On reaching the door, the woman who had assaulted her bent down, took off her high heels, and ran off. Through the window, the three friends watched her running down the street, stilettos in hand.

'Let's go somewhere quieter' Martin suggested. They finished their beers, leaving just as the police arrived. Two male officers intercepted them as they made for the door while a policewoman made her way towards the injured woman, still lying sprawled against the radiator, blood running down her face. One of the police asked them if they had seen what happened.

'Didn't see a thing, mate' Martin replied, and they exited the pub into light rain. Dadafarin was feeling a bit sick. He could feel the beer sloshing around in his stomach as he walked, and had a foul rotten metallic taste in his mouth. Before he had time to warn anyone, he vomited all over the pavement, causing a couple to veer away, but too late to stop the man's polished brogues from being splashed with vomit. The man started remonstrating, but a quick look at Igor made him scuttle away, cursing under his breath.

'I think I'd better get Dada back to the hotel' Igor said.

XXII
DADAFARIN GETS LEAVE TO REMAIN

Dadafarin woke up the next morning from a strange and very disturbing dream, covered in sweat. In the dream, Carey, wearing a long white dress with a sparkling tiara on her head, had been tied to a post on a stage outside the hotel. A large group of white men dressed like football supporters surrounded the podium, pointing and shouting at her. Behind her stood Donald Trump in a bright blue suit, smiling at the crowd and asking them over and over, in a loud voice, 'Shall I grab her by the pussy?', to huge cheers from the crowd. As Dadafarin slowly came round, with relief he realised that he was in his bed at the hotel, though he could still hear the sound of shouting. It appeared to be coming from outside his window, at the front of the hotel. He had a headache, and a foul taste in his mouth. The dream had left him feeling nauseous, or perhaps that was the beer he had consumed the day before. He could not remember anything from the trip to London after he had been sick, apart from a vague recollection of falling over in a train carriage and being helped onto a seat by Igor.

Getting out of bed, Dadafarin made his way to the window. Several vans were parked outside, and a number of police vehicles too. He could hear a number of refugees shouting, and a policeman had one of them in a headlock. Quickly, he brushed his teeth, splashed water on his face, put on his clothes. Relieved to find his 'phone next to the bed, he scooped it up, took his key card from the slot on the wall, and ran along the corridor and down the stairs rather than wait for the elevator. In the foyer was a group of about twenty refugees, standing in small huddles.

'They've taken Ibrahim!' Noureldine greeted Dadafarin as he walked into reception. 'The immigration authorities are taking people away, and Ibrahim is among them!'

Ibrahim, who out of all of them probably had the best reasons for needing asylum! Still feeling groggy, Dadafarin walked outside towards one of the police vans, and was intercepted by a burly policeman who told him to get back inside the hotel. In the rear of the van, he could see Ibrahim, dressed in white overalls. Quite why he had been dressed like this Dadafarin didn't know. He shouted out to Ibrahim.

'Don't worry, my friend, we will not let them send you back!' He could see that Ibrahim was in tears. Several others refugees sat despondent in the van with him. Dadafarin was shocked, and also disgusted with himself for feeling some relief that it wasn't him in the back of the van. Did this mean he was to be allowed to remain in Britain? A few of the refugees were shouting and waving their fists just outside the main door of the hotel, but most of them stayed in the foyer, evidently worried that any show of solidarity with the deportees could see them dragged away, too.

Dadafarin was pushed back towards the hotel, his last view of Ibrahim huddled disconsolately in the back of the van making him both angry and sad at the same time. How could Ibrahim, the gentlest person Dadafarin had ever met, be considered ineligible for asylum? A Muslim, he had stood up for Christians when they were being attacked by other Muslims. He spoke eight languages, had two degrees, and, out of the entire group of refugees in the hotel, had the most to offer Britain.

Back in the foyer, Noureldine described the morning's events. The immigration officials had arrived with a police escort at 5:30am, before anyone was awake. Some officers had surrounded the hotel, while others woke up those due to be deported. It was not long before the sound of shouting from a few of the refugees surprised in their room woke up others. A few of the refugees had run off, two of whom it turned out were not on the deportation list anyway. Ali was one of them.
'Go back to your room, Dada,' Noureldine advised Dadafarin. 'There is nothing to be done here.'

After returning to his room, Dadafarin curled up under the bedclothes, sad yet strangely elated at the same time. He only left his room for lunch, and was glad to find the dining room almost empty; there were only three men eating, none of whom he knew by name. He was relieved to find that he now had Martin's 'phone number stored in his 'phone; he didn't actually remember saying goodbye to him, let alone exchanging contact details. Taking advantage of the lack of people in the restaurant, Dadafarin made himself a few sandwiches so that he could skip dinner.

After dropping the sandwiches off in his room,Dadafarin took a brief walk in the grounds. It didn't help his mood, as he was reminded of his walks with Dr Venngloss. For the first time since his arrival, he felt very alone. He sat down on the grass at the bottom of the garden, took the 'phone out of his pocket, and, after a few moment of indecision, called Martin's number.

'Dada, that is terrible news' Martin agreed after Dadafarin had told him of the day's events. 'I still have some contacts in Antifa. One of them is an expert in social media campaigns. Maybe we can make this too embarrassing for the government. Give me a few days, I will talk to some friends. Do you have any photographs?'

Dadafarin remembered seeing Noureldine taking video or photographs with his phone. 'My friend Noureldine I think took some. I will call him and ask him to send them to me.'

The following morning, as he was leaving breakfast, Claire gave Dadafarin a letter that had just been delivered. It was from the Home Office. With pulse racing, he hurried to his room and tore open the envelope. His asylum claim had been successful. This wonderful news was tempered by his sadness over Ibrahim being taken away. What would happen to Ibrahim if he was sent back to the Sudan? He switched BBC News on to try and drown out the conflicting emotions that he felt.

Noureldine called Dadafarin a short while later to tell him that he too had been granted asylum. Dadafarin told Noureldine of his call with Martin, and asked if he had any pictures of the police arresting Ibrahim.

'Yes, and I think Ahmed took some too.'

'Ahmed? You mean the Moroccan guy?'

'Yes. I will call him. He was also one of the lucky ones. Let's meet downstairs for coffee in an hour.'

Over coffee Dadafarin in the foyer, gave Noureldine his own number as well as Martin's. Noureldine said he would send Martin several pictures that showed Ibrahim being arrested; Ahmed had also taken quite a lot of pictures before he'd been hustled back inside the hotel by the police. Noureldine also hoped Martin could do something, but he didn't seem very optimistic. He was going to go and stay with his relatives in Bristol. His cousin was picking him up in the morning. Ali had not been seen since the police had arrived, and no-one knew his whereabouts. There were rumours he had joined a religious cult based nearby. He was not answering his phone.

After talking awhile, the conversation became banal and slightly awkward, both men knowing that they were delaying the inevitable. It was time to say goodbye. As they both stood, Dadafarin offered his hand. Grasping his hand Noureldine pulled Dadafarin towards him and embraced him in a tight hug.

'You are a good man, Dada. Look after yourself.'

'You too, you crazy Syrian. Call me soon.'

Returning to his room, Dadafarin found that it no longer felt like home. The future beckoned, uncertain and a little frightening. The following day, he received a letter saying that he was to be rehoused in a halfway house in the nearby town, from where he could apply for benefits. It was time to get on with his new life. There was much to be done.

XXIII
DADAFARIN MOVES HOUSE

Dadafarin's new home was a six-bedroomed, run-down terraced house in the nearby town of Dorkton. The house was run by Clive, a jovial, bald middle-aged white man with tattoos all down his arms. He was very muscular, and looked like he had taken too many steroids. Dadafarin's fellow residents were a recovering drug addict named Sylvia, two prisoners recently released from the local prison, and two young homeless men who had been given temporary accommodation there by the local council.

Sylvia and the two released prisoners, Tony and Taj, were bound by conditions that limited when they could leave the house, where they could go, and who they could associate with. They also had ankle bracelets fitted so that they could be tracked. Tony was a thin, wiry white man, of around 50 years of age, with most of his teeth missing. He told Dadafarin, with some pride, that he had spent more than half his life in jail. Taj was a plump Asian man of around the same age, and spoke very little. Judging by the carved figures of Shiva and Buddha Dadafarin had noticed on a shelf in Taj's room one day, Taj was both a Hindu and a Buddhist.

Sylvia told Dadafarin she was twenty eight, though she looked twenty years older than that.

She had just come from a rehabilitation centre. Sylvia also told Dadafarin when he met her in the kitchen a few days after his arrival that Taj had just been released from a women's prison, where he had just finished serving a short sentence for fraud, or at least that was what he claimed he had been imprisoned for; Sylvia doubted that a fraudster would be tagged. Taj had told the authorities he was female shortly after his arrest, and his lawyer had persuaded the judge that his client could be seriously traumatised if sent to a men's prison. Dadafarin was shocked that Taj had evidently not made anywhere near the effort Carey had to become a woman; as a result, he became deeply suspicious of Taj, and avoided him for the rest of his stay. He hoped that no-one would think he was being racist or transphobic.

Dadafarin was given a musty smelling room on the second floor, with a threadbare carpet, a cupboard with a door that wouldn't stay closed, and a sink with a dripping tap that hung crookedly on a plywood board which had been nailed to the wall. An old television sat on top of a small cupboard, but when Dadafarin switched it on, it just emitted a hissing sound, with no picture at all.
It was a very depressing room, looking out over a busy street, and Dadafarin decided he did not want to live there. There were rumours of another lockdown, and he couldn't face the thought of being stuck in this dank and dreary room for months on end.

The day after his arrival, he called Martin. Martin had been busy.
'Dada, I have been talking to a friend of mine in Antifa. He thinks we may be able to make Ibrahim's story go viral.'
'Viral? You mean like coronavirus?' Dadafarin asked, confused.
'Well, not exactly, but similar. We can spread Ibrahim's story, bring it to the attention of the media and the public. We can mobilise protesters. Create hashtags that go viral. We can get it in the papers, on social media. We might even be able to organise a demonstration. We can make it impossible for the government to ignore. The pictures your friend Noureldine sent will help.'
'Ibrahim has more right to asylum than I do' Dadafarin said. 'He has more right than anyone who was in that hotel!' Dadafarin told Martin of Ibrahim's difficult journey to Europe. Martin agreed that this was indeed a grievous miscarriage of justice. He also admitted he was missing the excitement of his time with Antifa, and would welcome the chance to become politically active again.

Dadafarin felt a glimmer of hope. With the help of Martin and Lesley, maybe Ibrahim could be freed. Martin asked if Dadafarin was happy with him posting on Twitter using Dadafarin's account. He agreed, and said he would send his log in details via WhatsApp. Before they said goodbye, Dadafarin told Martin about his horrible, depressing room in the boarding house.

'Don't worry, Dada, everything will work out for the best in the end.' Martin assured him. 'You just concentrate on staying healthy. I will call you tomorrow.'

After his call with Martin, Dadafarin messaged Noureldine to thank him for sending the photographs to Martin. A few minutes later, his phone rang. It was Noureldine.

'Noureldine! How are you?'

'I am fine, Dada my brother. I am with my cousin. He is going to get me a job. But how are you?'

'I am OK. I do not like where I am staying. And I am very upset about Ibrahim.'

'Yes, Ibrahim is a good man. I cannot understand why they will not let him stay. I have sent your friend some pictures, and also some video. One picture shows Ibrahim in the police van. I will send them to you too if you like. What is your friend going to do with them?'

Dadafarin told Noureldine of Martin's plan. Noureldine tried his best to sound enthusiastic, but Dadafarin could tell by his voice that he obviously didn't think it would be successful.

'Good luck, brother!' Noureldine signed off, 'And keep me informed. Stay in touch!'

After speaking to his friends, Dadafarin felt depressed by the reality of the room around him. He had enjoyed speaking with Noureldine; in spite of his initial impressions, he now actually liked this crazy Syrian cannabis dealer. His phone pinged; Noureldine had sent a video and several photos on WhatsApp. Dadafarin watched the short video, which showed two of the refugees trying to drag another away from the officials who were escorting him to their van. He didn't know the names of any of them, but recognised Ahmed in one of the photographs Noureldine had sent.Two of the pictures showed Ibrahim sitting in the police van. In one of them, he looked visibly upset. After sending Noureldine a thumbs-up emoji, Dadafarin lay down on the bed, fingers clasped behind his neck, staring a stain on the ceiling and thinking about all that had passed since he arrived in Britain.

It had been a strange experience. He now knew that the freedom of the West that all the refugees had imagined was just an illusion. Britain was, in fact, broken. Racism, patriarchy, transphobia, fascism and climate change meant that life would always be a struggle, even here. It was quite depressing, yet, no matter how hard he tried, he couldn't shake off the feeling that perhaps there was something to be found in this country that the masses had somehow been conditioned to not see. The problems of systemic racism, transphobia and economic disadvantage in England somehow seemed very far removed from the oppression and violence affecting the countries he and his fellow refugees had fled. Everything is relative, depending on your point of reference, he thought to himself before dozing off.

XXIV
A DINNER INVITATION

The next day, Dadafarin decided he would go down to the local job centre in the hopes of finding employment. Although he had been told he could apply for benefits, he wanted a job. He still had some savings from the money deposited on his debit card every week, but he realised this would not go far, in spite of the recent increase of his benefit to £39.63. He already knew how expensive everything in Britain was from his previous outings.

Dadafarin decided that if he got a job, all the money he made would be used to help Ibrahim appeal against the decision to deport him. But first, he decided to call Lesley. Lesley answered almost immediately, on the second ring, and seemed very happy to hear from Dadafarin. They informed him that the appeal process was already under way for Ibrahim, along with those of eighteen other refugees due to be deported. Lesley also assured him that as long as the appeals process was running, Ibrahim would not be sent back to the Sudan. Ibrahim was being detained in a government detention centre, and Lesley hoped to see him within the next week. They would keep Dadafarin informed, and would pass on his best wishes to Ibrahim. Meanwhile, Dadafarin should enjoy his new freedom, and not worry too much. Lesley promised to keep him informed of the progress of Ibrahim's appeal, but warned that it might take some time.

A few days later, a very excited Martin called Dadafarin.

'Dada! Look on Twitter!' he announced excitedly. 'It's working! Ibrahim is going viral! Your tweet has been re-tweeted eighteen thousand times so far.'

'My tweet? I haven't been on Twitter' Dadafarin said, confused.

'No', Martin replied, chuckling. 'It means that the post about him I posted on your behalf is being re-tweeted on Twitter. Have a look, and call me back.'

'OK. I will call you back. What do I look for?'

'Search for the hashtag FreeIbrahim. And look on your own Twitter feed.'

After their call, Dadafarin signed in to Twitter on his phone and searched for the hashtag. And there it was! #FreeIbrahim was trending all over Twitter. The top post was under his own name, above the picture Noureldine had sent Martin.

"I was lucky. My gentle, kind and compassionate friend, Ibrahim, was not. An educated man, a teacher fluent in 8 languages, fleeing genocide in South Sudan, is somehow deemed a threat to Britain. Immigration officials removed him yesterday for deportation." Jerome Carbine, the ex leader of the opposition, and several other MPs had re-tweeted the post. It had been re-tweeted hundreds of times from a single account called The Anti-Nothing League, which had the two flags that Dadafarin now recognised as the symbol of Antifa.

A prominent black Labour MP, the Shadow Home Secretary Rihanne Bishop, had also re-tweeted his original post, with her own post stating "This governments egregilous (sic) immigration policies are killing people. I call on the Prime Minister to immedediatley (sic) reverse this unhumane (sic) decision. People cannot be disposed of like unwanted trash"

Dadafarin was ecstatic. The wonderful world of social justice in action! Dadafarin also noticed that he had received several direct messages, but the one that jumped out at him was from the greatest social justice warrior in the country, Jerome Carbine.

"Dear Dada' it read 'I am so pleased to see that your rightful indignation at the government's racist immigration policies is receiving so much support. I would like to offer what help I can. I would also like to meet with you to discuss it, if you would like. I enclose my secretary's number; please call her so she can arrange a meeting."

Dadafarin called the number straight away.

'Jerome Carbine's office' a woman's voice answered.

'Hello? I was asked by Mr Carbine to call this number' Dadafarin replied. 'My name is Dadafarin Engineer.'

'Dadafor what?'

'Dadafarin.' Then he remembered his Twitter handle 'Dada Engineer. I am a refugee. Mr Carbine sent me a message on Twitter.'

'Oh, Dada! Yes, Jerome told me to expect your call. It is so touching to see a refugee sticking up for his fellow asylum seekers. Jerome would like to invite you to dinner. Would next Wednesday be OK? We could send a car to pick you up.'
'Yes, I would very much like to meet Mr Carbine.' Dadafarin could barely contain his excitement. After giving his address, he was told to expect the car at five pm on Wednesday. Suddenly, the future looked bright again. He read all the other messages, all supportive, apart from a very nasty message telling him to "Piss off back where you came from, you ISIS cunt!" Why would anyone think he had anything to do with ISIS? He wasn't even a Muslim, let alone a female sex organ.

XXV
A DAY WITH NOURELDINE AND HIS COUSIN

The next few days passed in a blur. All Dadafarin could think about was his upcoming meeting with a man that, judging by his popularity with the social justice warriors, was seen almost as a prophet. Martin continued to run Dadafarin's Twitter account, and called him several times a day to discuss new tweets he was going to send. Dadafarin now had over seven thousand followers, and this was still growing exponentially. Justice in Exile were also very happy for the publicity, and Lesley had been it touch twice. On the second call, Dadafarin asked them about Carey.

'Carey is coming back to work next week' Lesley told him. 'She asked about you last time we spoke. I will tell her you were asking after her.' Dadafarin realised he was simultaneously disturbed and happy that he felt a twinge of excitement at this.

On the Monday afternoon, two days before his dinner with Jerome Carbine, Dadafarin was lying on his bed looking at Twitter when his phone rang.

'Hello?'

'Dada? How are you?' He recognised Noureldine's voice.

'Noureldine! I am fine, thank you. How are you?'

'I am very good. I am in London with my cousin,

and we would like to see you. What's your address?'
Dadafarin gave him the address. 'But it's not in London'
'Don't worry. We will be there in an hour,' Noureldine replied. 'We will take you out for dinner. Wait for us.' Before he could speak further, Noureldine had hung up.
Dadafarin could barely contain his excitement at the idea of going out. He paced the room until Noureldine arrived, wishing the time to pass. Life was looking up.

An hour later, Dadafarin's phone rang again. It was Noureldine.
'Dada? We are outside.' Dadafarin looked out of the window, and there was Noureldine, standing on the pavement next to a large black BMW saloon, with his phone to his ear. Noureldine waved. Dadafarin waved back, then gathered his keys and rushed down the stairs. Although at first he had disliked Noureldine, he had come to appreciate that Noureldine's brashness, his apparent rudeness, were in fact just aspects of his character. As they hugged on the street, in defiance of current Covid protocol, Dadafarin felt a wave of affection for this rough, tough street thug. He'd come to appreciate how difficult Noureldine's life had actually been in Syria, with factional fighting destroying most of the country, ISIS killing and kidnapping people as they tried to establish their caliphate, and a fascist dictator resorting to chem-

ical weapons and atrocities against civilians in his attempt to cling on to power. Small wonder that Noureldine had decided to seek a better life elsewhere.

Noureldine introduced Dadafarin to his cousin, Issam, a thin, short wiry man a few years older than Noureldine, dressed in a dark blue suit. Dadafarin noticed that Issam had several gold teeth, and wore what looked like a very expensive watch. Noureldine was also wearing a suit, though his did not look quite as well tailored as his cousin's. Noureldine insisted that Dadafarin sat in the front of the car with his cousin, and climbed into the back seat behind them. The car was obviously quite new, as it smelt of fresh leather. The interior was impeccably clean, and a tree-shaped air freshener hung from the mirror.

As they drove off, Issam still smiling as he expertly wove his way through the tight streets, Noureldine and Dadafarin exchanged news. Dadafarin told him about the campaign on Twitter to save Ibrahim, and his upcoming dinner with Jerome Carbine.

'Then we must buy you some new clothes' Noureldine said. He then launched into a rapid dialogue in Levantine Arabic with Issam, who smiled and looked across at Dadafarin.

'I know just the place' he said.

'But, I don't have money for clothes...' Dadafarin protested.

'You are our guest, and to refuse would be to insult

us' Issam replied, winking as he swung off a dual carriageway and down some narrow streets.

Thirty minutes later, they pulled up outside a small shop in Tottenham. It belonged to a Syrian Jew named Adam, who had fled the country many years earlier. He obviously knew Issam well, and announced he was very pleased to meet his favourite customer's cousin and friend. After trying on several suits, both Issam and Noureldine agreed Dadafarin looked best in a dark grey wool suit, and chose a black buttoned silk shirt to go with it. Dadafarin insisted he did not want a tie, as this was part of the uniform of white imperialists. Dadafarin told them he had read online that different coloured ties in fact often transmitted coded signals. Noureldine and Issam exchanged raised eyebrows at this, but agreed that he didn't need to have a tie. Dadafarin was embarrassed at being bought clothes, but how could he refuse? He knew that to refuse gifts from Muslims was often taken as an insult. After paying for the clothes with a credit card, Issam turned to Dadafarin.

'Do you like Syrian food?'

Dadafarin could not remember any specific Syrian dishes, but he was very much looking forward to some proper Arabic food. Although the hotel kitchen staff had varied the menu after all the complaints, and the food had improved dramatically after Noureldine had taken to visiting the kitchen, nothing could beat good Arabic food prepared by someone cooking their own culture's fare, in their own kitchen.

Twenty minutes later, they pulled up outside a restaurant called The Golden Fleece. The proprietor Ma'ashad, a rotund, balding, middle-aged man dressed in an apron over a pair of jeans and a greasy T shirt, shook their hands. Dadafarin had put his mask on, but was told to remove it.
'There's no Covid here' Ma'ashad reassured him. Ma'ashad evidently knew Issam well, and they hugged and kissed each other on the cheek, before Issam introduced Noureldine and Dadafarin. They shook hands.
'Ma'ashad makes the best foul outside Syria' Issam said.
They were ushered inside to a table. They were the only customers apart from a young couple sitting in a corner near the kitchen. Issam said a few words to Ma'ashad, and a minute later two bottles of beer and a glass of fruit juice arrived.

Noureldine poured the beer into glasses, handed one to Dadafarin, and proposed a toast. 'To freedom' he said.
'To freedom!' They both took a sip of their beer as Issam sipped his fruit juice.
'I thought you didn't drink?' Dadafarin asked Noureldine.
'I didn't. Not while I was seeking asylum. I was a pious Muslim refugee.' At this, Issam and Noureldine burst into laughter.
'But Issam, you don't drink?' Dadafarin asked.
'No. Not when I'm driving. They are much less

accepting of it here than they are in Syria' he answered, and the cousins both started laughing again.
'But, seriously now, what is happening with Ibrahim?' Noureldine asked. 'Will Ibrahim be released?'
'I don't know. I hope so' Dadafarin replied wistfully. 'I have started a campaign, as I mentioned. Actually, it is my friend Martin who started it.'
'And who is Martin?' Noureldine asked.

Dadafarin related the story of meeting Martin, and the party in Brixton. The cousins found it hilarious. He then explained about Martin's Twitter campaign to raise public awareness of Ibrahim's plight.
'Ibrahim is a great man,' Noureldine said, suddenly serious. 'He is the best of us all. And yet, he gets deported, and here we are, eating lunch in London. It is not right. If we can do anything to help, let us know, please. I will stay in touch with Martin. I would like to meet him.'

The food arrived; foul mesdames, salads, kebabs, grilled chicken, fresh flatbreads and hummus. Dadafarin had to deliberately slow himself down. The familiar tastes and smells, denied so long, gave him an appetite unlike any he had felt for months. The hummus was excellent. As they ate, Noureldine talked of his theory that hummus was tied up with religious extremism. The Jews claimed they'd invented it, he said, as did the Greeks and the Arabs. Nationalism, religious ideology and hummus all shared a viciously con-

tested identity, centred around Jerusalem.
'All these wars, they might as well be about hummus' Noureldine said. 'It doesn't make any sense. What is the difference between religion and hummus? With both, the recipes may be slightly different, but it's really all just the same thing.'

Dadafarin expressed his surprise that Noureldine was talking like this, especially since he had been one of the refugees vociferously complaining that the food in the hotel was not halal.
'English food is horrible' Noureldine explained. 'It is bland, they don't use spices. The only flavour they add is the weeds they call herbs. Did we not get better food when I helped in the kitchen? More familiar and tasteful food?'
Dadafarin had to admit that this had been a good tactic. The food had improved dramatically after Justice in Exile had intervened on their behalf and Noureldine had started assisting in the kitchen.

More beer arrived, and, as he mopped up the last of the foul on his plate, Dadafarin decided to ask Noureldine a question he didn't quite know how to put into words.
'Noureldine, I am so glad that you were given asylum. But....I...well...'
'Dada! Stop trying to be polite!' Noureldine interrupted. 'You want to ask why, when a pure and honourable man like Ibrahim failed to get asylum, was it granted to me, a Syrian cannabis dealer? I am not insulted by you asking, so please do not worry.' He picked up his glass, raised it, took a sip.

'It is a fair question.' He put down his glass, looked straight into Dadafarin's eyes.' You see, Dada my friend, I am gay.'

For a few seconds, Noureldine looked straight into Dadafarin's eyes with a look of earnest seriousness. A half-stifled laugh from Issam, and Noureldine's expression changed to one of mischief, as he and Issam burst into laughter. Issam was laughing so much that snot came out of his nose, his eyes pouring tears as he pushed his chair back and slapped his thighs.

'Yes, Noureldine is gay!' he exclaimed, and another bout of laughter consumed them both. Dadafarin was confused. Was this some sort of joke?

'Dada, don't look so serious' Noureldine admonished him. 'I had thought about wearing a dress to the Home Office interview' Noureldine continued 'but when I found the interview was to be in the hotel, I thought that I did not want you or the others to see me dressed like that.'

The cousins collapsed into fits of laughter again, Issam falling from his chair and knocking his juice over. The laughter was infectious, and Dadafarin now found himself joining in, even though he was still not sure that he quite got the joke.

'Noureldine is going to join Queers for Palestine!' Issam added as he took his seat again, trying to look serious.

'Queers for Palestine?' Dadafarin asked, confused. 'What is that?'

Wiping his eyes, Noureldine pulled out his phone,

and, after searching for a short while, showed Dadafarin a photograph of a group of men, some of whom wore dresses, holding a rainbow flag on which in large letters was written 'QUEERS FOR PALESTINE.'

'Hamas will welcome them to the struggle, I am sure' Noureldine said. 'But perhaps not in the way they imagine.'

Once again, Noureldine and Issam erupted in paroxysms of laughter. Noureldine, however, could sense Dadafarin was not quite sure to make of all this, in spite of it evidently being a joke. Dadafarin looked slightly bewildered.

Noureldine stopped laughing, putting his hand on Dadafarin's shoulder, serious now.

'No, Dada, I am not really gay. But I did tell the Home Office I was. I know that it's easier to get asylum if you are gay. If you are transexual, it is even easier, especially if you are from a Muslim country. But being a woman, that would be a step too far, even for me.'

'I would not like to see Noureldine in a dress' Issam added, and this time they all laughed.

'I met a transexual' Dadafarin told them after they settled down. The cousins both looked at him in surprise. He told them about Carey, and how sad he was that their friendship had been destroyed.

Both Issam and Noureldine found Dadafarin's description of how he had found out Carey was transexual hilarious, but both stopped laughing when they noticed how upset he was.

'Sorry, Dada, we should not laugh. If you love him, I mean her, what is the problem?' Noureldine said, much to his surprise. Noureldine continued, serious now. 'We are living in a new world, with new rules. If people want to be gay, or be a woman, who are we to judge? Who gives anyone the right to condemn others? Does it threaten them? No. Find your happiness, wherever that may be. But please just listen to one bit of advice. Do not believe everything you read, or hear from people who seem to have your best interests at heart. I feel you are a bit, as the French say, naïve. I only say this as a friend. You are a good man, but not all people who appear to be nice people actually are. There is a communist revolution going on, and the British and the Americans do not want to see it. They think it is justice, but underneath, it is just politics. It always is.'

On that sombre note, Issam signalled to Ma'ashad, who brought a small tray with the bill and some small, hard mints. Issam paid the bill with a wad of cash, leaving a large tip. They all said goodbye to Ma'ashad, who clasped both Dadafarin's hands in his and wished him luck in his new life. and then drove back to Dadafarin's boarding house. As they approached his new home, Dadafarin's mood fell.

'Come to Bristol and visit us soon, please' Noureldine said as they made their farewells. 'Maybe they'll throw another statue into the water.'

Dadafarin chuckled. 'Thank you, my friend. Thank

you very much. And thank you too, Issam. I have had a wonderful day.'

Issam hugged Dadafarin, then held him by the shoulders, forcing him to look into his eyes. 'And now, Dada, you are my friend too. I hope to see you soon. Here is my number. Call me if you need anything, anything at all. ' Issam handed Dadafarin a business card.

Farewells over, it was time for them to set off on the long drive back to Bristol. With a squeal of burning rubber and a blast on the horn, the two cousins disappeared into the evening traffic.

Dadafarin made his way up the stairs and back to his dismal room. The atmosphere of decay and poverty settled around him once more, making it seem almost as if the afternoon had never happened. However, as he hung his new suit in the musty wardrobe, he felt something in one of the pockets. Reaching into the pocket, he could feel a wad of paper. He pulled it out, and was astonished that it was money. He counted it out onto the bed, the crisp notes looking fresh and new against the stained cover on the bed. The cousins had slipped £500 into his new suit, evidently not wanting to embarrass him with the futile attempt to refuse their help. Dadafarin felt overwhelmed, and lay back on the bed and burst into tears.

XXVI
DINNER WITH THE INTELLECTUAL ELITE

Dadafarin felt quite nervous about meeting Jerome Carbine. He'd searched on the internet to find out more about him. Jerome Carbine had had a long and illustrious career as a Labour politician. His true socialist views, support for minorities, and incredible grasp of public opinion meant that he had eventually risen to be head of the Labour Party.

Dadafarin had been a bit surprised to find pictures online of Mr Carbine posing with members of Hamas. Hamas, Dadafarin knew, were not very nice people. There was even a picture from an old newspaper showing Mr Carbine with Yasser Arafat, the PLO leader who had sanctioned a number of hijackings. This open support of revolutionary Islamic groups was somewhat at odds with Mr Carbine's stand on gay and trans rights. It reminded him of Noureldine's comments about Queers for Palestine. Everyone from the Middle East knew that gay rights were not looked upon favourably by Islamist political groups. He decided that, if he got the chance, he might ask Mr Carbine about this.

On the day of the dinner, Dadafarin was ready an hour before the car was due to pick him up. He paced the room, checked his reflection in

the mirror, pleased at how he looked in his new clothes. He found he was checking the time on his phone continually. Finally, his phone rang.
'Mr Engineer? Your car is waiting outside' a female voice told him over the phone.
Making sure he had his keys, Dadafarin picked up his new jacket and made his way outside. A large black Bentley was parked on double yellow lines outside, evidently waiting for him. Somehow, he'd not been expecting a car quite like this. The driver, a large, friendly Caribbean fellow called Joe, opened the rear door for him.
'Can I sit in the front?' Dadafarin asked.
Joe agreed, and they set off towards London.

Traffic was surprisingly light. Dadafarin tried to make conversation, but Joe evidently didn't want to talk too much, beyond telling Dadafarin he was English, and, no, he didn't go to street parties in Brixton or listen to Hot Chocolate. An hour later, they pulled up outside a row of expensive-looking three storey town houses situated behind an ornate wrought iron fence.
'It's number 37. They're expecting you' Joe told him. Dadafarin got out of the car and walked to number 37. He was just about to ring the doorbell when the door opened. A dark-haired, slim, middle-aged white woman in a bright blue print dress stood there.
'Dada? It's such an honour to meet you!'
Dadafarin held out his hand, then realised that of course he could not shake her hand. Covid was

everywhere. However, he had immediately noticed that the woman was not wearing a mask. 'I am Doria' she continued, 'Welcome to my humble home!'

As Doria ushered him along a large hall lined with paintings of countryside scenes and horses, an ornate crystal chandelier hanging from the ceiling, Dadafarin wondered to himself if he quite understood the meaning of humble. He would ask someone later. Although he knew his English was actually quite good, there was always room for improvement. At the end of the hall, he was directed into a large room where a number of people were seated around a table. Dadafarin did not recognise any of the guests, apart from the instantly recognisable figure of Jerome Carbine. Dressed in a tweed jacket with leather patches on the elbows, untidy brown hair above a bearded bespectacled face, he wasn't quite the commanding figure Dadafarin had expected. Dadafarin admonished himself for remembering the tramp he had met in Hyde park. You cannot judge a book by it's cover, he had read somewhere. It was perhaps this look of plain ordinariness that the voters found so appealing.

Dadafarin had read a lot about British politics online. In spite of evidently being the most popular politician in Britain, judging by posts on Twitter, Jerome Carbine had received a devastating setback in the recent General Election of December 2019, when the working class, especially in the north of England, had proved to be too stupid to realise that the party that had always stood for them knew what was best for their future. The Brexit vote of 2016 had in fact given an indication of just how ignorant these people were, as the Labour Party had said publicly, but no-one had imagined just how successfully the bigoted flag-waving Conservatives had brainwashed the public into thinking that their best hope lay in a Tory government and a future outside Europe. Many Labour supporters, especially those in academia and the media, were convinced that Jerome Carbine had won the moral victory; this in spite of his own party ganging up on him after the election, then kicking him out of the party just because he didn't like Jews. Many of the refugees at the hotel didn't like Jews either, but no-one seemed to mind about that. Maybe it was because Mr Carbine was white, and therefore a racist?

'Dada? Or do you prefer Dadafarin?' Jerome Carbine stood up and proffered his hand, the slight trace of a smile on his lips. Dadafarin shook the legendary politician's hand, which unexpectedly felt limp and slightly damp. Surreptitiously wiping his hand on his trousers, he smiled back.

'It is such an honour to meet you, Mr Carbine. My friends all call me Dada.'

'Jerome, please. Only my enemies refer to me by my last name.'

'OK. Jerome. '

'Let me introduce you to everyone, Dada.' Jerome

then introduced Dadafarin to Andrea, his wife, a slight, timid looking woman. Cecilia, a large-boned woman in a voluminous turquoise dress shook his hand firmly, in contrast to Basil, a black man in glasses, who like Jerome had a very limp handshake. Dadafarin wondered if this limp handshake was a secret signal, like the special handshake Whip had told him that the Freemasons used. A slight middle-aged woman in a tight dress was introduced as Claire.

'And, of course, you've already met Doria' Jerome continued. Another woman, younger than the others, was never introduced, and Dadafarin never did find out her name. 'Boner is in the other room, admiring some paintings Jerome added. 'But let me get you a drink. What would you like?'

'Well, some wine would be nice' Dadafarin replied, noticing several open bottles on the table.

'White or red?' Andrea asked.

'Red please.'

After his wine was poured, Dadafarin was invited to sit next to Basil. He immediately sensed that Basil did not like him. Ignoring Dadafarin as he took his seat, Basil casually paged through a book he just taken from the bookshelf behind him. It seemed quite ignorant behaviour. Basil was black, so racism could not be the reason. Was Basil jealous of him somehow? Perhaps he felt his elite minority status was somehow under threat. They had similar scores on the matrix of identity, thought Dadafarin, though Basil was evidently

English as opposed to his own foreign origin. No matter, he was not here to meet Basil.

Excusing herself, Doria went into the kitchen to prepare the food. A tall, thin, very pale and gaunt man, dressed completely in black and with long black hair, walked in from an adjoining room. Andrea introduced the man to Dadafarin. 'Dada, this is Boner. Boner, meet Dadafarin.'

Boner strode over, grabbed Dadafarin's hand in a crushing grip, and pumped it violently.

'It's a real honour to meet you!' Boner exclaimed, in a strong accent that Dadafarin recognised as being Irish or Scottish. Or perhaps Welsh; Dadafarin still had a lot of difficulty with accents. He had spoken to a man from Glasgow when buying toiletries from the filling station near the hotel, and at first had assumed the man was speaking a foreign language.

'I have heard so much about you' Boner continued 'It's wonderful how you are campaigning for your friend.'

From the look on Boner's face, he was evidently expecting Dadafarin to know who he was.

'Boner is from the band 3' Jerome explained.

'Three? Sorry, but I don't listen to pop music much.'

A slight scowl crossed Boner's face, but he grabbed a glass, poured himself a wine, and proposed a toast. 'Freedom from tyranny!' he said, raising his glass. They all drank to that, then Andrea disappeared into the kitchen to help Doria prepare din-

ner. Jerome took his seat at the head of the table, and then asked how the campaign to free Ibrahim was going.
'Well, on Twitter it is going very well. My friend Martin has been most helpful,' He told them about Martin, and how he had met him. This was met with an embarrassed silence, broken eventually by Basil.
'Well, you've got important friends now'

Boner then proposed another toast, this time to friendship. Dadafarin noticed a patch below Boner's nose that looked like talcum powder. Judging by his rather restless behaviour, Dadafarin realised it was more likely something else.
'Martin is a very important friend to me' Dadafarin said.
'Quite. But I doubt he has the same influence we have' Jerome replied.
Dadafarin refrained from pointing out that, if not for Martin, none of them would ever have met him. He wasn't here to make friends, anyway. All that mattered was freeing Ibrahim.

They were interrupted by Doria asking from the door to the kitchen if Dadafarin ate meat. 'I made sure we had no pork' she added.
'Yes, I eat meat. Pork too.'
Basil took this opportunity to announce that Boner and himself were vegans. 'We cannot use any animal products' he explained.
Dadafarin already knew this, because many vegans on Twitter evidently thought it necessary to re-

mind everyone of their dietary preferences whenever they tweeted. The way Basil had said it sounded like he was trying to score points, or was betting on a hand of poker. Dadafarin had been taught how to play poker by his uncle. If Basil wanted to play stupid games, so be it. All that was at stake was Basil's ego.

'A bit like the Jains' Dadafarin remarked, raising the stakes slightly. He would wait to see what Basil's next play was. He very much doubted Basil had any idea what he was talking about.

'Jains?' Basil enquired, on cue.

'Jains wear cloth over their mouths.' Boner interrupted. 'In case they accidentally swallow an insect.' Everyone looked at Boner as he continued 'They are like totally committed vegans. I've thought about doing that myself. Being a Jain.'

Was Boner really trying to play a hand in their game of intersectional poker? A white middle-aged man? Surely not?

'So what led to you fleeing Iran?' Boner asked, as he refilled Dadafarin's wine glass.

'I am from a persecuted minority. The Ayatollahs don't like my people.'

'Are you Sunni?' Jerome asked. 'Sectarianism is so unnecessary.' Jerome evidently knew a bit about the demographics of Iran. But then again, he did boast a close friendship with several leading Muslim clerics, both Sunni and Shi'a.

'We all worship the same God, in the end' interjected Basil, looking a bit bored and bemused.

Ashamed at himself for the childish thrill he felt at playing a winning hand in their game of intersectional poker, Dadafarin looked closely at Basil before replying. 'I am Mazdayasna. Zoroastrian. It is not the same God.'

Basil folded, leaning back in his chair and picking up his glass of water.

'How fascinating!' It was the first time Cecilia had spoken since their introduction. 'Didn't Nietzsche write a book about that?'

'Not exactly, no. ' Boner interjected. 'Thus Spake Zarathustra is not about Zoroastrianism. It is about truth and morality. Nietzsche merely used Zarathustra, or Zoroaster, to illustrate his idea that man is just a bridge between the animals and what he called the *Übermensch,* or Overman.'

'Sounds like something a Nazi would say' Basil commented, evidently peeved that he had been beaten at his own game.

'The Nazi's co-opted Nietzsche for their own purposes' Boner replied. 'But the whole book is full of contradictions. I think it can be interpreted in many ways. I found it very difficult reading.'

'Nietzsche is considered by some to have committed great blasphemy' Dadafarin added, surprising everyone. 'He declared that God is dead, which really says both that God exists, but that he has no power over the fate of man.'

'So it is not really about Zoroastrianism?' Cecilia asked.

'No, it is not.' Boner interjected.

'So what is Zoroastrianism? Are you polytheists, or you believe in the same God as Christians, Hebrews and Muslims? One God?' Cecilia enquired.

'We believe in one God.' Dadafarin explained. 'The ideas of heaven and hell were taken from the Zoroastrian religion. In fact, not just heaven and hell, but also that concept of one God. Also Satan, the duality of good and evil, and even the concept of the soul, all these came from my religion. The idea of your Judgement Day also comes from Mazdayasna. All of these ideas were stolen by the Abrahamic religions, and then we were displaced. Many followers were forced to convert to Islam. Others were declared infidels, and were enslaved or killed. Even the Christians did not protect us. There are not many of us left.' Another embarrassed silence ensued, which thankfully was broken by Doria announcing that dinner was ready.

Dinner was a selection of vegetarian dishes, mostly salads. Some rather nice looking home-made pickles were dotted around the table in small china dishes. Doria had provided a plate of cold meats for the unfashionable meat-eaters. Dadafarin couldn't help notice that Jerome didn't talk very much, and looked perpetually upset. Claudia and Cecilia seemed far more interested in each other than anyone else. Everyone seemed to treat Dadafarin with deference, as if he were a spiritual leader or something. Basil had slouched back in his chair; he ate little, occasionally picking at the selection of salads on his plate. Conversation was muted while they ate.

When Doria brought in cake and tea, Boner asked Dadafarin what his plans were now that he had been granted leave to remain.

'I would like to start a small farm. I prefer the countryside, I think. City life is not for me. If I could find a small piece of land somehow, Ibrahim and some of my other fellow refugees could join me, and we would grow vegetables and be self-sufficient.'

'That sounds very noble' Boner replied 'Perhaps I can help out. Meanwhile, tell us about your friend Ibrahim.'

Ibrahim's mistake had been to be too honest, Dadafarin explained. His admission that he had helped the smugglers find people to fill their dinghies had been seen as complicity in their crimes. In fact, Ibrahim had been fleeing certain death in the Sudan. Dadafarin related Ibrahim's story, which moved Doria to tears. They all seemed upset. Jerome Carbine promised to take up the matter personally, and Boner said he would like to help out too. Things were looking up, perhaps.

After dinner, the guests discussed the current state of politics in the UK. None of them seemed to like the new leader of the Labour party, Sir Byn Stormer. Apparently, Jerome held the moral high ground, and everyone knew it, in spite of the election results. The collapse of the so-called Red Wall in the north of England was entirely the fault of Brexit. In spite of the Labour Party repeatedly telling their traditional voter base that they were too stupid to understand what Brexit really meant, the people up north just didn't seem to get it. What could you do when your own supporters didn't understand what you were telling them?

Doria seemed to have taken a shine to Dadafarin, evidently enhanced by the bottle of wine she had drunk since he arrived. She swapped seats with Claire, who had been sitting on his left, when Claire went to the toilet. Doria's hand kept touching Dadafarin's leg under the table, lingering longer than manners dictated. It was making him uneasy. Doria was old enough to be his mother, and surely her behaviour was not really appropriate? It somehow seemed a bit wrong, and the thought of Doria naked was not very appealing anyway. However, it had been a long time since Dadafarin had lain with a woman, and perhaps he was just being ageist?

Dadafarin was snapped out of his daydream by Boner.

'Dada, I have an idea. How would you like to go and stay on my farm in Yorkshire. You could help out on the farm. You would be paid for any work you do. You said you were a motorcycle mechanic? I am sure you would get to grips with farm machinery very quickly.'

A burst of excitement and gratitude filled Dadafarin. He could feel his heart pounding in his chest, and stopped breathing momentarily as he took in Boner's words.

'Yes, please, that would be wonderful. I have worked a little on tractors before, in Iran. Yorkshire? Where is that?' Dada asked.
'It's up north. The heart of Labour. Or it was' Boner replied, smiling sardonically at Jerome. 'You'd be welcome to stay as long as you like. We have an accommodation block for the seasonal strawberry pickers from Romania. This season was a disaster for strawberries, due to the travel bans, so the block hasn't been used this year. You can invite your friends, when they can travel. You could have the whole block to yourselves.'
'Oh yes, that would be wonderful! I really don't like living in the town.'

After some further discussion, it was agreed that Dadafarin would be picked up the following week. Meanwhile, he would let Lesley know and find out what paperwork was involved in him moving from his provided accommodation. He felt really excited for the first time since arriving in Britain. This was his destiny, he knew it.

XXVII
DADAFARIN GOES FARMING

Dadafarin arrived at Coldshott Farm in a downpour in mid September. He had been picked up at his boarding house that morning by a driver sent by Boner. The previous day, Dadafarin had gone shopping in Dorkton, buying himself underwear, three pairs of jeans, several shirts, a fleece, a sturdy pair of boots and a waterproof jacket. The driver, Lennie, kept Dadafarin entertained on the journey with stories of his wife, three young children, two dogs and four cats. Lennie owned a small farm in Kent, not far from the Georgian Hotel, and drove private hire vehicles to make ends meet. Before Dadafarin's departure, Lesley had assured him that they would take care of all the paperwork involved with him moving home, while expressing delight that Boner had taken it upon himself to help Dadafarin in his new life. Lesley had been especially moved when Boner sent them a signed CD of 3's latest album, Blood On The Cross. Dadafarin had also been given a copy, at the dinner, but Lennie having announced himself to be a big fan of 3 on the drive up, Dadafarin decided to give him his copy. He would ask Boner for another one, or see if he could download the album.

Coldshott Farm lay just outside the village of Woodkirk, near Batley in Yorkshire. The farm buildings and house were all built from cut stone blocks. At one end of a yard littered with old trailers and farm machinery stood the house, a large two storey building with bay windows. Next to the house was a large shed with wooden walls to half the height of the roof. The farm was surrounded by fields and, in the distance, a forest could be seen through the rain. They pulled up in front of the main house and Lennie got out of the car, opened the rear door for Dadafarin, and retrieved his bag from the boot. Dadafarin looked in his bag and presented the CD Boner had given to Lennie, who was very happy to receive it. Strangely, he asked Dadafarin to sign it. As they said their goodbyes, a young man with spiky red hair wearing overalls and purple Wellington boots approached from one of the sheds attached to the main building.

'Ar reet' he said. 'You bin Dadafarin, ah reckon?'

'Dadafarin, yes. But my friends call me Dada.' Dadafarin had only recognised his name in whatever the young man had just said.

'Ah, OK, Dada. Less ger theurr inside. Ah'm Garriston. Um call uz Gary, but ah prefers uz full name.' They shook hands. Garriston's grip was very firm, and he didn't release Dadafarin's hand until he'd locked eyes with him for a few seconds. His eyes were a piercing blue, and Dadafarin had the bizarre feeling that Garriston was taking a look at his soul. He hoped he'd passed whatever test this was.

Garriston took Dadafarin's bag and ushered

him into the main house. They entered the kitchen, which had bare stone walls, a large stove in one corner, and a huge wooden table. Garriston invited Dadafarin to sit on one of the ancient wooden chairs arranged haphazardly around the table. He then busied himself filling a kettle with water and placing it on the stove.

'Let's av um tea. Can theur cuk?' Garriston asked, putting teabags in a couple of large mugs.

'Cook? Not really.'

'Tha's eur shame' Garriston replied, 'I'm pretty bad a' it, mesell.'

Dadafarin realised that Garriston was making a great effort to enunciate his words so that he could understand them, but still had trouble making out exactly what he was saying. He felt honoured to immediately be invited to drink tea, which he understood to be a very important social ritual from the few episodes of Eastenders he had watched.

'My friend Noureldine is a very good chef, but I have never really tried it. But I would like to try.' Dadafarin replied.

Garriston's phone rang, and he had a conversation in what to Dadafarin sounded a foreign language. He made out a few words, including tractor and field, but the rest was totally unintelligible. After hanging up, he turned to Dadafarin.

'Dada, I av ta nip on. Mek yersen a 'ome' Garriston then grabbed some keys from a sideboard and rushed out of the door.

Garriston came back a few hours later. In the meantime, Dadafarin had looked in the kitchen cupboards and the refrigerator, mindful of Garriston's enquiry as to whether he could cook. He noticed that there were few womanly touches about the place, and wondered if Garriston was gay. He certainly didn't display any of the simpering femininity he had noticed many gay people seemed to adopt, presumably as a way of identifying themselves to each other. On a shelf near the stove, he found some cookery books, and resolved to cook dinner with whatever he could find. He had no idea when to expect Garriston to return, so decided to have dinner ready for 6 o'clock, which was his best guess as to when most English people seemed to eat dinner, judging by the few soaps he had watched on television at the hotel. This gave him three hours to try and match what food he found in the kitchen with one of the recipes and cook it. He thought about looking online for a video on cooking, but discovered his phone had no signal. He also couldn't find any evidence of a Wi-Fi signal, in spite of what was obviously a router in the hallway. Eventually, he decided on a recipe and busied himself preparing dinner, having to substitute a few ingredients with similar items.

Dadafarin had just finished cooking when Garriston walked into the kitchen. Garriston was surprised and very pleased to find dinner waiting for him. He told Dadafarin that he had planned to take him to the local pub for dinner, but they would do that another night. Currently, they could get two meals for the price of one under the government's Eat Out to Help Out scheme. Garriston said it was the first time he had ever eaten curried pork moussaka, but he appeared to enjoy it very much, having two extra helpings, both of them washing dinner down with a tasty dark beer which Garriston said he had made himself.

During dinner, Garriston told Dadafarin, annunciating his words carefully so that he could understand most of it, that his father had been a farmer, but when he died, the farm had had to be sold to pay taxes to the government. Boner had bought the farm, then taken him on as manager. Initially, he had been paid half the profits in addition to all his bills being paid, but due to the terrible weather the previous year, the farm had only turned a profit of £217. Garriston was now paid a salary, in addition to his share of the profits, should there ever be any. Dadafarin was shocked to hear that dying in Britain was such an expensive pastime.

'Isn't it strange, managing what should have been your farm?' Dadafarin asked.

'Shit 'appens. Boner is eur reet gran lad. Knows fuck orl abaht farmin' mind, bur 'e looks affer uz' Garriston replied, swigging down the last of his beer. Dadafarin was shocked to hear Garriston referring to someone twice his age as 'lad', but assumed it was a local colloquialism.

After dinner, Garriston showed Dadafarin

to a room upstairs, furnished with a sagging double bed, a battered wooden chest of drawers and a wardrobe without a door. In spite of the room's tired appearance, Dadafarin liked it immediately. He had been expecting to stay in the uninviting Portakabin block he had seen as they drove into the farm. Garriston pointed out the bathroom, just down the hallway.

'Do you have the internet? I don't have any 'phone signal.'

'No, lad, sorry. The line is brok. Anotha lad wor wukkin 'ere till las' week, 'e dug up the fibre-optics while diggin up blocked drain cos if 't rain we bin 'avin. Should be fixed soon, mind.'

Disappointed that he could not get online, nonetheless Dadafarin was very pleased with his room. Outside the window, he had a view across a slate roof to the farmyard and the trees in the distance. He could see a hairy black and white dog in the yard, looking up at him and wagging it's tail. He would introduce himself to the dog in the morning. Dadafarin unpacked his meagre possessions, putting them neatly in the cupboard, before brushing his teeth and crawling under the duvet. Feeling tired and contented, he soon fell asleep.

XXVIII
BONER VISITS WITH HIS SON

Over the next few months, Dadafarin discovered that farming was hard work. The farm covered two hundred and fifty acres, with a mix of arable and dairy farming, though currently they only had thirty cows. Strangely, Boner got paid by the government for not farming some of the land and letting it go wild instead. The cows had to be milked twice every day, and this was the first job that Garriston taught Dadafarin, though Carl, a young man from the village, came to help in the mornings. In addition to milking, the cows feed had to be constantly replenished, their pens mucked out and fresh straw laid down. When out in the fields, the cows knew when milking time was, and made their own way to the shed as long as the gates were opened for them. The dog he had seen outside was called Shep, and had been a sheep dog when the farm had sheep. Shep wasn't allowed in the house, but soon he was accompanying Dadafarin on his daily work. They quickly became firm friends, and Shep would even jump in a trailer when one was hitched to one of the tractors.

The farm machinery was relatively straightforward mechanically, but one of the two tractors had a cockpit that reminded Dadafarin of space ships he had seen in Hollywood science fiction films. It was made by Lamborghini, the Italian sports car manufacturer, and had eighty-four buttons, thirty-two gears, and a computer. It would be a month before Garriston would risk letting Dadafarin use it in the fields. However, Garriston was very impressed when Dadafarin fixed a cultivator that had broken down the year before. Using a tig welder, Dadafarin replaced a part of the machine with one he fabricated from bits of metal found lying at the back of a barn. Dadafarin also serviced the much older and simpler Massey Ferguson tractor, and was happy driving it, but he was still struggling to come to grips with the Lamborghini. Garriston decided to set aside two hours a day for a week to teach him. After Dadafarin had learnt how to drive the Lamborghini and operate the machinery on both tractors, he was soon out in the fields. His first sortie in the Lamborghini was with a huge hedge cutter, trimming back the hedges. He loved this tractor, which had air conditioning, a radio and even Bluetooth.

The whole of October was so busy that Dadafarin had not left the boundaries of the farm once. Shopping was delivered weekly, and much to Dadafarin's delight, Garriston would happily eat anything presented to him. In November, the cows needed supplementary hay, and they still needed milking twice every single day. Things always needed mending, and most of the day was spent fixing farm machinery, fences, and anything else that required maintenance. The day started at six in the morning, and at 5pm he headed back to the farm to cook dinner. After dinner, it was milking time again. Dadafarin went to bed completely exhausted at 10pm, just to repeat the whole process the next day. By the time he felt he could take a few hours off to visit the village, the entire country was in lockdown again.

Dadafarin started taking brief walks in the countryside with Shep when he could, just for a change of scenery. Shep loved these walks, and always picked up a stick to carry with him. Farming was not quite the idyll Dadafarin had imagined, but he found he did not mind the hard work. He was getting very fit, and the routine of the farm stopped him worrying about things. His only entertainment apart from television was his frequent phone calls with Martin, though he had also started exploring Boner's library. The phone reception at the farm was terrible; the only place that Dadafarin had found where he could get a signal was on top of a haystack, in a field adjacent to the farmhouse.

One day on a call with Martin, Martin announced that Ibrahim's GoFundMe page had passed £10 000 so far in donations. Martin had also run into Carey when he had been to see Lesley at Justice in Exile. Carey had told him that she would like to see Dadafarin again. Dadafarin had mixed feelings about this; while he really liked Carey, and still thought of her often, he was afraid that she might still want to have sex with him. Try as he might, he could still not come to terms with the idea of intimate relations with someone who had a penis, even if they were female.

Martin told Dadafarin that Jerome Carbine couldn't ask questions in Parliament any more, as he had been suspended by his party for anti-Semitic statements, but he had apparently been lobbying his friends in government on Ibrahim's behalf. On Twitter, the initial storm of support for Ibrahim had now died out, swallowed up in Twitter's never-ending litany of causes, campaigns, hashtags and cancellations. It wasn't sounding good.
'Oh, and your picture was in the papers' Martin told him.
'In the papers? How?' Dadafarin asked.
'That dinner you went to with Jerome Carbine. It got in the papers, because Jerome Carbine had broken the rule of six. There were eight of you there. The article didn't have your name, just your picture with them at the dinner. I'll send you the picture later.'

After saying goodbye to Martin, Dadafarin called Noureldine. Noureldine said he was starting a new business, though he didn't want to discuss it over the phone. He promised to visit as soon as travel was allowed. Just after this call, he received a WhatsApp message from Martin. It showed him at the dinner with Jerome Carbine, sitting next to Basil, looking straight at the camera. He remembered Boner taking a picture on his 'phone, and wondered how it had got in the papers. There had actually been nine people at the dinner; apparently none of the papers seemed to realise that the picture was most likely taken by a ninth person.

Life on the farm wasn't quite the idyll Dadafarin had imagined, though he found that he actually enjoyed the hard work; he now felt fitter than he had ever been. He had come to grips with the space-ship tractor, and much preferred it to the old Massey-Ferguson. Technically, he could not legally drive the tractor on the roads to get between the fields, but Garriston had never asked if he had a driving licence. Dadafarin often listened to Radio 2 in the tractor, and also caught up on the news while ploughing, spraying or drilling the fields. There was talk of the lockdown being temporarily lifted for Christmas. Currently, a tier system was in force, each tier having different restrictions, but Dadafarin had no idea what tier the farm was in. He never left the farm, all the shopping being delivered weekly. Dadafarin was responsible for ordering the shopping, but this mainly involved just ordering the same items every week. He could now cook a different meal for every day of the week. Garriston would eat anything presented to him, so he was not under any pressure to produce gourmet meals. As far as Garriston was concerned food was just fuel, and as long as it kept them going, that's all that mattered.

Over dinner one night, Dadafarin asked Garriston why he wasn't married.

'Don av t' time. T'would be grand to have eur lass an all that, but ah don't have time to meet 'em. I'd like bairns, bur not afowa they's owd enough ta 'elp on t' farm. They'd jus' be dead weight, like' Garriston replied, chewing on a chicken drumstick. 'Boner's allus on 'bar it. Oh, 'e's comin' up tomorra. And t'internets fixed.'

Dadafarin was pleased to find out that he could now get back online. He'd been out of touch with the world too long. Boner had not been to the farm since Dadafarin's arrival, and he was looking forward to seeing him again. Hopefully he would have news of Ibrahim. He'd seen Boner on the television once, talking about Palestine. Maybe Dadafarin could ask him about pay? Since he'd arrived on the farm, a salary had never been mentioned. He still had the money Noureldine and Issam had given him, however, and with no way of spending it he wasn't unduly concerned about his finances.

Late the next afternoon, a Saturday, Dadafarin had just parked the Lamborghini when he heard the sound of a helicopter. He watched as a bright blue helicopter landed in the field adjacent to the farmhouse. At first, he thought it was the police helicopter he had seen passing overhead a few times, but then he recognised Boner as he alighted from the machine, clutching a large box. Dadafarin climbed down from the tractor and walked across to meet him. With Boner was a pimply youth who appeared to be in his late teens. Both crouched down as they ran from the blast of the helicopter's rotor.

'Whisky!' Boner shouted, holding his hat as the

helicopter took off and turned away. 'And I bought some scones from Fortnum and Mason's. It's to celebrate the harvest.' The young man with Boner had his hands in his pockets, and didn't look very happy to be there. He looked like a younger version of Boner, except he slouched and his long dark hair was unkempt and greasy-looking.

Boner embraced Dadafarin, then introduced the youth standing next to him. 'Dada, this is my son Vee. He's come to help on the farm for a while.'

'V? Like the letter?'

'Yes, that's right. Spelt V double E. ' the young man said, smiling. 'Nice to meet you, Dada. I've heard a lot about you' They shook hands.

'Let's get inside' Boner said.'Is Garriston here?'

'He's gone into the village' Dadafarin replied.'I saw him drive off a while ago. He should be back soon.'

Dadafarin was confused by Boner's mention of celebrating the harvest, since he knew that the harvesting had been finished shortly before he'd arrived. It was now late November. Boner apologised for not coming sooner, citing the lockdown.

'But then, I realised I could come for a business meeting.'

The three of them went into the kitchen. Boner cracked open a bottle of whisky, took three shot glasses out a cupboard, and poured them all a whisky.

'Here's to freedom!' Boner said, raising his glass.

He'd proposed the same toast at Jerome Carbine's dinner, Dadafarin remembered. They all raised their glasses and took a sip. The whisky burnt Dadafarin's mouth, and he almost spat it out. It had a strange taste, like dirt.

'Did you hear the news?' Boner asked. 'Ibrahim cannot be deported, at least not for a while. His appeal is going to the High Court. The High Court tend to look favourably at appeals, I am told. Fingers crossed.'

'Fingers crossed?'

'Yes, fingers crossed. It's for good luck.' Boner held up his crossed fingers to show Dadafarin, who grinned and copied the gesture.

'Fingers crossed!'

'I am sure his appeal will be successful. I've got my own lawyer on the case, helping your friend Lesley' Boner reassured him. 'Once Ibrahim is released, he can join you here if he likes. Oh, did I mention that I am leaving Vee here? I would appreciate it if Garriston and you could show him the ropes on the farm. He already knows how to drive the tractors. And please, don't let him leave the farm on his own. He'll just end up buying weed in the village.'

'Of course,' Dadafarin said. 'It would be my pleasure.'

Vee scowled at his father. 'I'm not a kid any more' he protested.

Dadafarin was overcome with joy at the idea of Ibrahim joining them on the farm. He had not

heard from Lesley for a while, but then they didn't seem to use WhatsApp. He raised his glass.
'To freedom!'

Between the three of them, they had finished a bottle of whisky before Garriston returned. Garriston and Boner greeted each other like long-lost friends, opening another bottle. It looked like they were all going to regret this in the morning, Dadafarin thought to himself. He cooked spaghetti bolognese while Boner told them tales about touring with his band. Vee went to his room after dinner, saying he was tired. After Vee had left, they ate the scones, Garriston and Boner arguing about which should be put on the scone first, jam or cream. Dadafarin was then instructed, as a neutral observer, to try both methods, but left the discussion stalemated when he said he couldn't really tell the difference. Boner asked Dadafarin to tell them about his adventures in London; the story of Martin and the street party had both Boner and Garriston in stitches of laughter. Later on, Boner brought an acoustic guitar through from the lounge. He gave a rendition of 3's signature anthem, Broke and Broken. It sounded terribly sad. After that it all got a bit hazy. Dadafarin had meant to call Martin, but he was too drunk. It could wait until the morning.

Dadafarin woke the next day with a pounding headache to the sound of a helicopter taking off. He made it to the window just in time to see Boner flying away towards the south. He hadn't asked about his salary. Looking at his phone, he realised he was a bit late for work.

XXIX
THE FIRE TEMPLE

A few days later, Dadafarin asked Garriston about his salary.
'Salary? That's for Boner ta sorts art. 'e doesn't kna owt abaht brass, e's sa much of it. Probably never occurred ta 'im. Ah'm sure e'll soart it art. Don' worry abaht it. We wor all eur bit drunk last neet. Whoa is this Carey lass theur were callin' abaht? I'd like to meet her.'
Dadafarin wondered exactly what he'd said about Carey. He felt an unexpected pang of jealousy that another man might be interested in her, and it made him feel uncomfortable. Dadafarin remembered very little after Boner had picked up his guitar.

After a quick breakfast, Dadafarin fed the chickens and let them out, then finished work on a plough he had been repairing. Then it was off to spray the winter wheat before milking time. He got back to the farmhouse at four pm, to find Vee sitting at the table in the kitchen.
'Hello' Dadafarin greeted him.
'Hi.' Vee looked tired, and seemed not to want to communicate.
'Have you eaten?' Dadafarin asked him.
'No, I'll wait for dinner, thanks.'
'So are you not in school?' Dadafarin continued.
'Nah. I got expelled. Hated it anyway. School's full

of wokey twats' Vee replied.
'Wokey twats? What are those?' Dadafarin had heard the word twats before. He understood it to be a swearword used to describe people you really didn't like.
'Social justice warriors.' Vee continued. It was the first time Dadafarin had ever heard this said in a derogatory tone.
'What were you expelled for?'
'Othering' Vee replied, grinning. 'Can you believe it? I told a teacher who accused me of othering the black students in my class that I was in fact the one being othered. Because I am white.'
Dadafarin was extremely confused. What on earth did 'othering' mean? Sensing Dadafarin's confusion, Vee explained. 'Othered, and othering, is when someone brings attention to the fact that you are different. Makes you stand out, so that the mob can turn on you. So by their rules, I got othered.'
'That sounds horrible. But how could someone 'other' a white person? White people are privileged.'
Vee looked aghast at Dadafarin. 'You really believe that crap?' Vee asked. 'It's Iran you're from, right?'
Dadafarin was feeling distinctly uncomfortable.
'Yes, Iran'
'Are you religious?' Vee enquired. 'A Muslim?'
'No, I am Mazdayasna. Zoroastrian. But not a very good one. I haven't been to a fire temple for years.'
'Zoroastrian? Fire temple? That sounds cool. Boner

was going on about Zoroastrianism once, something to do with a book he was reading. Maybe we could build a fire temple?' Vee suggested.

'I'm not sure your father wants a fire temple on his farm' Dadafarin replied, frowning. He found it odd that Vee referred to his father by his first name. It implied a lack of respect, he thought. 'And it would not be possible' Dadafarin continued. 'Even the lowest grade of sacred fire, the *Atash Dadga,* has to be consecrated by two priests. I have not met a single Zoroastrian since arriving in this country, let alone priests. And I am not qualified to look after a temple.'

Vee wasn't listening; he was getting carried away with the idea of a fire temple.

'He'll love it!' Vee continued, smiling. 'Anything that sounds a bit unusual, especially if it's spiritual, and he'll be right in there' Vee reassured him. 'He spent a month in a Buddhist monastery in a Nepal. I bet he could find you a couple of Zoroastrian priests.' Vee then announced that next summer, they would build the temple.

In spite of not really believing that this would ever happen, Vee's reference to the future made Dadafarin feel a bit more secure.

Later, as they made their way back to the farmhouse after milking, Vee suggested they go the village pub.

'Oh no, I couldn't' Dadafarin replied. 'I'm always so tired nowadays, and we have to be up at 5 o'clock tomorrow.'

'Come on. I bet you've not been out since you got here?'
'No, I have not even been to the village yet. Are the public houses even open?' Dadafarin asked.
'Yes, but we have to eat a substantial meal, according to the latest edict' Vee replied. 'So, let's skip dinner and eat there.'
'Are you old enough to go to a pub?' Dadafarin asked.
'Not really, not for another few months. But they all know me here. No-one will say anything.'
Why not, Dadafarin thought. Garriston had gone out on a socially-distanced date he'd organised on the newly restored internet, and had said he wouldn't be back for dinner. A night off from cooking would be a pleasant break.

XXX
VEE AND DADAFARIN GO FOR A SUBSTANTIAL MEAL

After showering, Dadafarin found Vee waiting downstairs in the kitchen. Vee informed Dadafarin had asked Carl, the occasional farm helper, to milk the cows that evening, as neither of them knew when Garriston would return. They left a note for Garriston in case he returned before they were back, and then walked into the village. On the walk to the pub, Dadafarin commented to Vee that it must be exciting growing up as the son of a rock star. With sadness in his voice, Vee told Dadafarin that his mother had died when he was four. With his father spending so much time away, his youth had been spent with a succession of nannies, relatives, friends and even, for a whole summer holiday, a stint living with a childhood friend of his father's who ran a circus. He had then be sent off to boarding school at the age of twelve. However, he thought has father had done the best he could under the circumstances, and it meant that he had had a very interesting and thorough grounding in life.

'I could have ended up woke otherwise' Vee said. 'What a disaster that would have been.'

This revelation left Dadafarin feeling slightly uncomfortable. Why would Vee think being woke was such a bad thing?

The village had two pubs, but Vee said the Red Lion had the best atmosphere, and were less likely to ask him for ID. The Red Lion was an imposing old thatched building situated at the top of a hill, on the main street of the village. It looked like a picture from a postcard, if you ignored the warning tape around a large hole in the street just outside. As they walked into the bar, the buzz of conversation they had heard from outside suddenly died away, and all eyes turned to them. Being a Tuesday night, the pub was not very busy, and all the clientele, apart from one middle-aged couple, seemed to be rough-looking men on their own. Recognising Vee, a few called out greetings, and the hum of conversation resumed.

Finding an empty table, Vee and Dadafarin removed their masks, and almost immediately a rotund bald man of about fifty years of age wandered over to their table and muttered something that would have sounded to Dadafarin like a foreign language a few months ago. Vee asked for two pints of bitter. It didn't sound very appetising, but Dadafarin was all for trying out local delicacies. However, on seeing the menu, written with chalk on a large blackboard next to the bar, he soon changed his mind about sampling local flavours. Just below the starters of soup or prawn cocktail, written in bold chalk letters, was written:

Todays Special
FAGGOTS, MASH AND PEAS £7.95

Dadafarin was shocked. Martin had told him that the people 'up north' were a bit strange, even claiming that they had sexual relationships with sheep, but he had not mentioned homophobic cannibalism. Suddenly, Dadafarin had lost his appetite. He wondered where the rump steak listed just below the faggots had come from.
'I'm not hungry' he told Vee.
'But you have to eat. It's a requirement to eat a meal if we want to drink beer.'
'But they've got human meat on the menu' Dadafarin objected, pointing to the blackboard.
Vee looked at him in shock, but when he saw where Dadafarin was pointing, he chuckled quietly. 'Nice one, Dada. You almost had me.' However, when Vee looked back at Dadafarin, expecting to see a smile, he soon realised he was deadly serious. Vee burst out laughing, causing several pairs of eyes to swivel in their direction.
'Sorry, Dada. I shouldn't laugh. Faggots are like meatballs' Vee explained, wiping tears from his eyes. 'They're made of pork. They're actually usually called ducks in these parts, but visitors would be confused, so they're called faggots here in this pub.'

Dadafarin looked at Vee in astonishment. He'd rather eat a duck that wasn't than a faggot, he thought to himself.
'Ducks?' he exclaimed. 'Why would they call pork meatballs faggots, or ducks?' Martin was right

after all. These Yorkshire “folk”were indeed very strange.
'Faggots existed long before it became a homophobic insult' Vee informed him. 'In fact, one day I had a discussion about it in here with Garriston. It's the Americans who started using it as an insult to gay people. Garriston thinks their co-opting of the word shows gross disrespect to British culture.'
Dadafarin, now better informed, said he agreed with Garriston. 'I should have known better' he told Vee. 'I once ate Bombay Duck, and that turned out to be rotten fish!'
They both laughed, and Vee signalled to the barman that they were ready to order. Dadafarin still decided to go with the safe option of fish and chips.

While they waited for their dinner, Dadafarin asked Vee how he felt about being expelled from school, just before sitting his final exams.
'I don't really care. I don't need their education. It was crap anyway' Vee said, picking at a beer mat on the table. 'It was one of the first of the private schools to introduce Critical Race Theory as an integral part of the curriculum. Of course, they're all it now, even the state schools. It was all very inclusive.'
'What was the school named?' Dadafarin asked. He'd seen something in the papers about a teacher from Eton being sacked for harbouring fascist anti-inclusive views.
'The American College of London. They are very progressive. They even let us decide what to study,

up to senior school. Anything we wanted. I'd thought my dad was paying for other people to educate me, not for me to educate myself. It was a bit like a cult. Have you ever had really religious people smile at you like they know the answer, and they know you don't?'
Dadafarin nodded.
'Well, most of the staff, and many of the students, they didn't even give me that smile after a while. They thought I was dangerous.'
'Dangerous? How could you be dangerous?'
'I didn't think like them. I didn't believe that men could be women, and that the world was structured around white patriarchy. I had a few friends, but we were ostracised by most, even those we knew agreed with us. Most students were scared to say anything, because daddy would be pissed off if they made waves. The last thing someone who moves in art or film circles wants is to be publicly shamed by his unwoke kid. Anyway, one day in a maths class we were discussing the role of white supremacy in mathematics. Karen, our maths teacher, had a new book she wanted to show us, called "A Pathway to Equitable Math Instruction-Dismantling Racism in Mathematics Instruction." Bill Gates had financed it through his foundation with a million dollar grant.'
'Maths is racist? Really?'
'According to Bill Gates. The book had only just been introduced into schools in California, Ohio, Georgia and Oregon in the States. Karen had man-

aged to get hold of a copy from a friend of hers. Apparently, expecting students to come up with correct answers perpetuates white supremacy. Before discussing the book in more detail, Karen said she would like to invite the students to speak of their own experiences, to discuss the social structures that had led to white supremacy taking over science. First, two of the black students stood up and talked about how they were subjected to racist micro-aggressions constantly. One of them, a Caribbean lad called Winston, had been insulted recently when a white girl asked after an English class if he understood Milton's poem "Il Penseroso". Then a Korean girl, Ye-Jun, said that people looked at her funny because she looked different. Actually, she was pretty hot if you ask me. I think they just fancied her.'

Vee paused for a long draught of beer, wiping his lips on his sleeve before continuing .
'A friend of mine, Kwaku, was asked if he had any comments' Vee continued. 'Kwaku refused to speak. Kwaku was from Ghana, and was actually quite open about his contempt for woke ideology, but this was generally dismissed by the teachers as a cultural issue. Kwaku had however recently upset several students and teachers during a discussion about slavery during a student debate: he told them that his Ashanti ancestors had been slave traders long before the Atlantic slave trade started, and had continued selling slaves long after Britain had stopped the trade. Kwaku had added

that he wasn't proud of it, but he refused to accept any guilt on behalf of people who had died long before he was born. Carla, a non-binary "Latinx" girl from California, was so upset by this that she had to go to the safe space.'

'Safe space? What is that?'

'The safe space was a room full of soft cushions. Minority students were encouraged to use it when they felt they'd been othered, or at any time they needed to escape from anything that upset them. Straight white students weren't allowed in there.'

'So what happened to make them expel you?' Dadafarin asked. He still wasn't sure why Vee had hated the school so much, but for the first time Dadafarin realised that being white might not always be as advantageous as it seemed.

'Well, I was getting bored with the woke stuff' Vee continued. 'It was becoming very fashionable. I was probably the only student in the class without any woke points. As far as I remember, apart from the three straight black guys, we had two gays, a trans girl, two non-binaries and a lesbian in the class. These kids knew nothing about real life. They spent most of their life on Instagram."

'I have not seen much of Instagram' Dadafarin said. 'Is it like Twitter?"

'It's basically Twitter with more pictures. All the so-called "influencers" use it' Vee explained.

Dadafarin had seen a lot about influencers online, but had not ever got round to starting an Instagram account.

'Sorry. You were telling me why you got expelled.' Dadafarin was now listening in rapt fascination. He had had no idea that social justice had been incorporated into the education system.

Vee signalled to the barman for more beer before continuing. 'Well, Carla stood up next and spoke about the difficulties of non-binary pronouns. Then May, the trans girl, spoke about the trauma of being misgendered. She was taking female hormones, though she had been on puberty blockers for years before that.

'Puberty blockers? What are they?' Dadafarin asked.

'They stop puberty. You know, when boys start growing hair and their voice changes, and girls grow tits.'

'That sounds terrible.' Dadafarin was shocked. He wondered if Carey had taken these hormones. Perhaps that is why she looked like a woman, he thought. 'And is this legal? They let children take drugs to stop them becoming adults?'

'Yes, it's legal. It doesn't stop them growing, it just stops them becoming sexually mature. Although May did look like a thirteen year old boy, even when wearing a padded bra. She was going for gender reassignment surgery next. There's a charity called Mermaids that actively helps children who want to change sex. May was once trying to raise money for them in the school.'

'I didn't know about this.' Dadafarin announced in surprise. 'I just thought transgender people already looked like the opposite sex. But sorry, continue. What happened next?'

The barman brought two more beers, and they both took sips before Vee continued. 'After May had spoken, the white boys in the class were invited to talk about their privilege. An American dude called Sky then told us how ashamed he was to be descended from genocidal white settlers. This was a bit strange, as he was a first generation immigrant. I knew the teacher wasn't going to invite me to speak, but I insisted.'

Vee paused for another another gulp from his beer. Dadafarin was having trouble keeping up with him, and was starting to feel a bit tipsy.

'Reluctantly, Karen let me speak. So I stood up and announced to the class that I wished I was black. If I was black, I wouldn't be expected to stand in front of the class and apologise for my dad marrying his childhood sweetheart and having a white kid. Then I walked out of the class. Initially, I was suspended from classes. Sky was apparently so traumatised on black people's behalf that he refused to ever go in the same room as me again. I was accused of othering the black people in the class by trying to project my own racism onto them. So the school othered me, and I was asked to leave. Dad wussed out and accepted a refund for the whole year. Though, to be fair to him, he doesn't blame me. He blames himself for not being more active in his role as a father.'

'Wussed out? What does that mean?'

'No balls' Vee grabbed Dadafarin's testicles under the table to make his point. Dadafarin recoiled, banging his head on the wall.

'See. You're too uptight, and you seem a bit woke yourself. Dad told me he thought you were, anyway. For all his faults, he's not stupid. How come you're falling for all this shit? How did a refugee from Iran end up woke? Especially one who appears as well educated as you?'

Rubbing his head, Dadafarin leant forward, unconsciously crossing his hands in front of his crotch.

'When I came to this country, I was treated with great kindness' he explained. 'When I met Dr Venngloss, I was very impressed by his, you know, desire to help others, at the expense of his own privilege.'

'Selflessness is the word you are looking for.'

'Selflessness? OK. What a nice word. I will remember that. Dr Venngloss reminds me of what you Christians call a saint. Well, he was like that. I don't know what has become of him.'

'I'm not a Christian. And who is this Dr Venngloss?'

Before Dadafarin had a chance to answer, the meal arrived.

XXXI
VEE'S THEORY OF WOKE

The fish and chips was excellent. After they had eaten, Vee ordered more beer by signalling to the barman. While they waited for the plates to be cleared and the beer to arrive, Vee asked Dadafarin about his life in Iran. Dadafarin told his story, from his life in Iran to his arrival in Great Britain, a country he had held in high esteem since childhood. He told him of Dr Venngloss, and the good doctor's fall from grace, and was shocked that Vee seemed to find it amusing. Vee sometimes seemed to be an ignorant bigot, though Dadafarin found he couldn't help liking this unusual and outspoken young man.

Sensing Dadafarin's disgust at his reaction to Dr Venngloss's cancellation, Vee squeezed his arm. 'Dada. Don't take everything so seriously. You are free, you have a place to live, and you can still think your own thoughts. Don't be so quick to believe that anyone who is nice to you has your best interests at heart. Your own country is an example of what happens when an ideology takes over. And, believe me, woke is an ideology. In fact, it's a religious ideology.'

Dadafarin suddenly felt uncomfortable, and didn't really want to continue the conversation further. But he was fascinated that a privileged young white man thought like this. Vee, in spite of his apparent bigotry, actually seemed highly intelligent.

'Religious?' Dadafarin asked. 'How can it be religious? They have no God. They don't have temples, or churches, or even priests.'

'They have plenty of priests. They're all priests. Robin DiAngelo and Ibram X Kendi are their prophets. The God they worship is an idea. Their religious texts are the sacred writings of Critical Race Theory. Their religious services are the pulling down of statues, marching with placards, or piling onto someone on Twitter. Have you looked into their eyes when they're talking to you? The really woke ones have the look of the zealot about them.'

'I think you're a bit crazy' Dadafarin observed 'But I have noticed that woke people get very angry with anyone who disagrees with them. And I have often wondered why being called white became an insult, and how black men like Officer Tatum on YouTube are actually white, and white people can't be black, but men can be women. I met a man who was a woman. But the people will be less angry when society is more fair. It will all settle down when everything is better.'

'Better?' Vee exploded, snorting loudly. A few heads in the bar turned. 'It will never get better. Are you familiar with Critical Race Theory?'

'A little. I've seen a lot about it on Twitter, and Dr Venngloss explained some of it to me. Dr Venngloss said White Fragility is a good and sim-

ple explanation of it. After I had read it, I thought strange that it was written by a white woman. Perhaps must hate herself.'
'You've read White Fragility?' Vee asked, evidently surprised.
'Yes. My friend Carey gave me a copy. It is a very interesting book.'
'White Fragility is basically Critical Race Theory for dummies' Vee continued. 'It's for people who can't actually understand the elaborate language that the academics deliberately use to make people think they are being profound. It sounds like you've been infected.'
'Infected?' Dadafarin exclaimed with horror. 'What do you mean, infected?'
'With woke. Critical Race Theory. It is basically malware' Vee explained. 'You know, like computer malware?' Dadafarin nodded, confused.
'Like all malware, CRT was not designed with good intentions' Vee continued. 'It is like a rootkit. It was designed to hijack and corrupt the part of the brain that deals with empathy. Similar to how religion operates; the difference is that most religions were not started with bad intent. CRT attacks the part of the mind that is emotionally concerned with the common good. The empathetic response. Morality is largely moderated by the same circuits. CRT came from universities, and the woke variant in public circulation is a stripped-down version.'

Dadafarin's brain was beginning to hurt. How had a seventeen-year-old boy with white

privilege come to these conclusions?
'Where did you read this?' Dadafarin asked. 'And why would anyone develop something that attacks people's minds?'
'I didn't read it, specifically, anywhere. It was the conclusion I came to by reading, studying teachers and staff at school, and by looking on social media, especially Twitter. Twitter is the front-line of the culture wars. With the limited amount of characters you can use, people are forced to put down what they think in simplified form, so it tends to distil their thoughts. They can't use as many of the obfuscating words they would normally use.'
'Obfuscating?' Dadafarin interjected. 'What does that mean?'
'Obfuscating means to intentionally make something harder to understand.' Vee explained. He was getting quite animated now. Dadafarin was fascinated.This was not the same slouching pimply adolescent he had first seen getting off Boner's helicopter.
'But what about gender?' Dadafarin asked.'How does that fit into all this? Gender has nothing to do with race.'
'It follows the same narrative, of oppression and victimhood. Do you know what an avatar is?' Vee asked.
'Yes, I think so. Like a character in a video game?'
'Yes, exactly. On Twitter, Facebook or Instagram, everyone is an avatar. They can say things they wouldn't normally say in real life. Nowadays, es-

pecially with the pandemic, people can end up spending more time online than in the real world. Eventually they *become* their own avatar. That's why it's so easy for a man to imagine he is a woman. Online a man *can* be a woman, or even a new gender entirely. A weakling can be an alpha male, a she a they, a him a her. With intersectionality, minority status is everything, and there is a vast smorgasbord of identities to choose from. There is a hierarchy of victimhood. You know about intersectionality?'

'Yes, Dr Venngloss explained it to me. What is a smorgasbord?''

'A smorgasbord is a like a buffet. Like food at a party.' Dadafarin nodded his understanding.

' Well' Vee continued 'a white male, the lowest form of life on the intersectional scale, can get treasured woke points if they are non-binary, genderqueer, or just some identity they've seen on TikTok. That's why so it's trendy to have pronouns nowadays; gender identity is a road to salvation. Where their whole world falls down is race. Race is the one identity in woke that is sacrosanct.'

'Sacrosanct?'

'Sacrosanct means sacred, too blessed and pure to be interfered with. Although CRT claims race is a social construct, the woke's actions indicate otherwise. If it is just a social construct, as gender is, then why can you not choose to be black? After all, a man can be a woman. But in a world based entirely on subjective ideas, contradictions do not matter. To an avatar, reality is the illusion. The woke have become figments of their own imagination, inhabiting an imaginary world, a world of pessimism, where everything is rotten.'

Vee paused and looked at his 'phone, which had been making beeping noises since they arrived in the pub. Dadafarin looked stunned.

'There is a revolution going on' Vee continued, in a quieter, almost resigned voice, 'and no-one is really paying attention. Most of the people fighting in it don't even know it's happening. They are just drones, reprogrammed to be the foot soldiers of the revolution. The aim is the destruction of Western society. They are not rewriting history to make it fairer and more inclusive, they are trying to erase it. Trigger warnings in books or on old TV shows are not out of concern for the consumer, they are to put the consumer off ever reading or watching it in the first place.

'But why?' Dadafarin asked.

'They want to create a post-modern Marxist utopia.'

'Utopia? What is a utopia?'

'An imagined perfect society. Impossible to achieve, of course, because no utopian fantasies ever take account of human nature, which is based around ego.'

Dadafarin was shocked. It was the first time he had heard any sort of argument against woke apart from some comments by cynical fascists on Twitter. Dadafarin didn't really understand all Vee had said, but much of it seemed, in his drunken state, to make perfect sense. He had a strange sensation of vertigo and felt slightly nauseous; whether this was the beer, Vee's words, or a combination of the two, he wasn't quite sure. His mind was reeling, not just from the beer, but from the evident sincerity of Vee's belief in what he was saying. Dadafarin's sense of uneasiness was not helped when he became aware that a man on the other side of the bar kept staring at him.

'CRT is not new' Vee continued. 'It has a long history. It's based on ideas from Marxism, and postmodernist theories that started in Frankfurt in the 1930's. The Frankfurt School. You should look it up. These ideas migrated to France with academics fleeing the Nazi's, and then to America after Hitler invaded France. The Americans developed it into Critical Legal Studies in the 1970's. Critical Race Theory developed from that....'

'Please, Vee, can we talk about something else? I'm feeling sick...' Dadafarin was now having trouble following what Vee was saying, the words fading into the soft hum of other voices in the bar. The man seated across the room was still staring at him.

'Sorry, Dada, I get carried away sometimes' Vee apologised. 'I just find it so crazy that anyone falls for this crap.' Vee could sense Dadafarin's discomfort. Dadafarin looked bewildered, and a little ill.

Vee sat back in his chair, sighing. 'Anyway, let's pay and go back to the farm' he suggested. 'We can drink some of that whisky.'

Vee picked up his beer, which was still half full, and drank it all in one go. He then signalled to the barman, who was busy pouring beer with studied concentration, a smile on his face. Dadafarin left half of his beer unfinished. Vee insisted on paying. Dadafarin waited in the porch while Vee exchanged a few pleasantries with some of the customers in the pub, and they set off back to the farm.

XXXII
WHO THE FUCK IS SID?

It was raining outside, a soft, cold drizzle made a metallic orange colour by the street lights. The damp breeze revived Dadafarin a little, and he looked forward to the walk back to the farm.

'So how do you like working on the farm?' Vee asked, as they left the shelter of the bar's porch.

'I really like it. I hope I can stay for a while' Dadafarin replied wistfully. 'It is very kind of your father to let me stay.'

'I'm sure you can stay as long as you want' Vee reassured him. 'Boner has a good heart. He's not been the best father, I hardly ever see him, but he means well. Besides, Garriston told me you are a great help on the farm. He really likes you.'

Dadafarin felt a warm glow of pride in this revelation. Garriston's opinions, and he had many, seemed to mostly come in unexpected statements totally unrelated to whatever was going on around him, but he always spoke his mind. Dadafarin really did like working on the farm. He desperately wanted to stay, and decided keeping Vee onside was probably wise. Besides which, Vee being around added a welcome bit of variety to the daily routine. Dadafarin realised he had almost forgotten how much he enjoyed other people's company.

Dadafarin was just about to speak when someone called out behind them. They both turned round to see a grinning figure walking towards them. It was the man who had been staring at Dadafarin in the bar. Dressed in jeans and a T-shirt, skinny with thinning unkempt dark hair, he was obviously drunk, swaying unsteadily on his feet, a wide grin on his face.

'Sid! 'The man exclaimed, then belched loudly. 'How the devil are you?'

Vee looked around, wondering who the man was addressing. 'Who the fuck is Sid?' he asked. The man was looking directly at Dadafarin.

Excuse me?' Dadafarin enquired 'I don't know you.'

'It's me, Olly' the man replied, sticking out his hand.

Dadafarin kept his hands in his pockets. 'Sid? Who is Sid?' he asked.

'Sid? You're Sid! Come on! We met a few times in Leeds. At the university. We went to Manchester together once, to see Asylum. Great gig, that. They've broken up now. Are you still in the Hare Krishnas? Guess not, seeing as you're here.'

'You must be mistaking me for another person, I am afraid' Dadafarin replied, looking confused. Vee was looking at both of them, his eyes flicking from one to the other.

'What's the problem, mate?' Vee asked the man. 'My friend is not from Leeds. He's Iranian. I don't know who the fuck Sid is, but this isn't him. Piss off.'

'No need for that!' the man exclaimed. 'I know this guy. He was studying at Leeds University while I was there. I'd know him anywhere. He was studying history, always tinkering with an old motorcycle he'd picked up somewhere, a BSA I think it was. Said he was going to ride round the world on it. He took too much ecstasy, dropped out and joined the Hare Krishnas. Last time I saw him, he was dressed in orange robes, banging cymbals in a park with a group of them. He didn't want to talk to me then either. I thought he'd been brainwashed.'

'You're mistaken' Dadafarin said. 'My name is Dadafarin. I have never been to Leeds.'

'Yeah, right' the man replied, before belching loudly.

'Go on, mate. Piss off' Vee repeated.

'Fucking weirdo' the man replied, looking at Dadafarin. He then turned away and staggered back towards the bar, muttering to himself as he tried to light a cigarette in the drizzling rain.

XXXIII
WHISKY, AND A SONG IN THE LEADROOM

Back at the farm, Vee opened a bottle of whisky. They settled in front of the stove in the kitchen, which was still burning, small flames licking the last of the wood Garriston must have put in it before going to bed.

'So, what do you think that was all about, that guy who thought you were someone called Sid?' Vee asked, as he filled two shot glasses.

'I don't know' Dadafarin replied. 'I must look similar to someone with that name. They say everyone has a twin, somewhere. It is very strange, he seemed so certain I was someone else. But he was very drunk.'

'You're not actually Sid, are you Dada?' Vee said, looking straight into his eyes. 'You're not just pretending to be a refugee, are you?'

Dadafarin laughed, raising an eyebrow as he looked back into Vee's eyes. 'Why would I give up a secure life in Britain, to pretend to be someone seeking asylum? Why would I risk deportation to a country I'd never been to, in order to remove myself from the benefits of being a citizen here, with no guarantee of being successful in my application? I'd have to be crazy. They could have sent me back to Iran.'

'Yes, you would have to be crazy' Vee replied. 'It's

just that the world is so crazy now, anything's possible. But I really like you. You seem, underneath all that woke shit, to be a genuinely good person. So, let's talk no more of craziness, and instead, drink to a better future. But you really must change your reading habits. You've filled your mind with crap. Boner has some great books. Have you heard of Douglas Murray?'

'Yes, he's a fascist isn't he?'

'No, he's not a fascist. Read his book, The Madness of Crowds, and then we'll talk again. Maybe it'll open your eyes to all this woke stuff a bit. There's a copy on the bookshelf in the lounge. Meanwhile, here's to free thought!'

'To free thought!' Dadafarin replied.

They talked late into the night, about religion, Iran, music and films. It turned out they both liked the Rolling Stones. Vee was very surprised that Dadafarin had watched Citizen Kane. His uncle had somehow obtained a copy, Dadafarin explained, and half the village had come round to his parents' house one night to watch it, on the huge new TV his uncle had just given them. Movie nights became a regular event in the Engineer household, with guests bringing snacks and drinks. On another occasion, they had watched Apocalypse Now, Dadafarin revealed. He had then read Joseph Conrad's book, Heart of Darkness, on which the film was based; Farside Contractor had given him a copy. It was this book, Dadafarin said, that had first alerted him to the true horrors of colonialism. The whole book turned out to be, in retrospect, about white supremacy, which is one of the reasons why Dr Venngloss's pronouncements on modern Western society had resonated so much.

'There's a new colonialism afoot' Vee said. 'The colonialism of thought. And it's perhaps even more dangerous, because it is less obvious. It does not use weapons, just words. There's a new tendency towards authoritarianism, in business and government. Have you heard of the World Economic Forum?'

'Yes I have, but I don't know much about them. I thought it was all a conspiracy theory.'

Dadafarin remembered Whip talking about the World Economic Forum. After realising how absurd it was to think that people could be controlled by radio signals through an implant, Dadafarin had assumed that most, if not all, of what Whip had told him had been nothing more than paranoid fantasies. It all sounded like a James Bond film, with Klaus Schwab and the WEF playing the parts of Blofeld and Spectre.

'Martin's friend Whip said that they were going to take over the world with a program called the Great Reset.' Dadafarin added. 'Is it true, then?'

'Yes' Vee assured Dadafarin 'well, the Great Reset is real. Klaus Schwab has even written a book about it. The WEF want a cashless economy with governmental controls. It all sounds nice until you realise how easily this can be attached to a social credit system like they have in China. Emmanuel Macron, Jacinda Ardern and many other senior members of world governments are graduates of the WEF's Young Global Leaders Forum. Justin Trueau has given seral speeches at the WEF. Ardern and Trudeau have already implemented authoritarian government, using Covid as the excuse. But look it up yourself, and make up your own mind. It is not my intention to persuade you of anything. It seems enough of that has been done already. It's all on the WEF's own website, they aren't even trying to hide it.'

'So do you think the World Economic Forum are behind the social justice movement?' Dadafarin asked.

'No, Dada, I don't think so. Woke ideology came from the universities, although Ibram X Kendi has just signed up with the WEF Young Global Leaders. But critical social justice started long before the WEF. The WEF are just cashing in on social trends. They say they support LGBT and human rights, but they also promote companies based in Saudi Arabia and China. Members of the Bahrain and Qatar royal families are in the Young Global Leaders program, so it's hardly based around equality. But enough of the WEF's ideas intersect with critical social justice for them to make common cause, and they actively support many of the same agendas. Basically they all want a form of Marxism. But it seems the WEF are hedging their bets, as their article on CRT shows.'

'Hedging their bets?'
'Waiting to see what happens, so that they can distance themselves from it if it all goes wrong.'

Vee poured them both another shot of whisky before continuing. 'The immediate problem I think is woke ideology. The schools, universities and the media have now all been infected by ideology, which means that a small percentage of the population are controlling what is being passed off as public opinion. Most members of the public who don't go along with these ideas are scared to speak up. Words like racism, transphobia, and now even white, have been weaponised. And they are very effective weapons. No-one wants to be labelled a racist, or a homophobe.'

Dadafarin sipped his whisky, studying Vee carefully. Was Vee just another conspiracy theorist, or was he in fact a very clever young man? He showed every bit as much conviction as Dr Venngloss had when talking about social justice, but Vee's arguments somehow seemed more coherent, less vague.
'So how did you end up thinking like this?' Dadafarin asked. Although he did not really want to talk any more about social justice, he couldn't help but be fascinated by this young man and his unusual ideas.
'Observation mostly, and my own research' Vee explained. 'I have always been inquisitive; it got me in a lot of trouble while I was growing up. The first BLM demonstrations alerted me to the fact that

something unusual was happening in society. In the middle of a pandemic, suddenly thousands of people were on the streets and everyone, including the government and the media, seemed to forget Covid for a day. Also, school seemed to be becoming less about education, and more about indoctrination. My friend Kwaku lent me Gad Saad's book The Parasitic Mind, which compares ideas to pathogens. It made a lot of sense, I thoroughly recommend it. But I came to my own conclusion that woke wasn't really a pathogen as such, it's more like a computer virus.'

'So if this is indeed a virus, as you say, what is the tool to be used to remove it. The antivirus?'

Vee seemed to consider his answer carefully for a moment before replying. 'Free speech, and the courage to use it. People need to be less gullible, see past the slogans and buzz words. Check everything for themselves. In an age where more information is available to the average citizen than there has ever been, I find it strange that people don't make more use of it. No offence, but look what happened to you.'

Dadafarin felt a bit offended by this last comment. 'What do you mean, look what happened to me?'

Vee poured more whisky. 'Sorry, Dada, I don't mean that in a bad way. You are a good person, but I think that you are a bit naïve, but at least you seem to have an open mind, and you question things. You are actually the first person I have spoken to about all this in such depth apart from Kwaku. Many don't want to look beyond the hype. People need to open their eyes. Parents need to understand Critical Race Theory, but not the version brewed in university laboratories. Academia is of no use to the average person. Besides which, it's academia's fault woke ideology escaped into the world at large. All this should have been discredited years ago. But no-one needs to understand Hegelian philosophy, or know who Foucault is. They don't even really need to understand Marxism. They only need to understand the woke ideology being taught to their kids.'

'Hegelian? Foucault? I've never heard of either of those' Dadafarin said. He now felt very drunk.

'Hegel and Foucault were philosophers. Both have influenced woke ideology, especially Foucault. But that is irrelevant to anyone outside academia. People need to act, not babble on about where ideas came from. Silence is complicity. The silent majority can't wait four years between elections to make themselves heard. A lot can change in four years. People need to stand up for what they think is right. That is what I am going to do, with music.'

Dadafarin was now wishing Vee would stop. His whole body felt tense, he could feel his pulse throbbing in his temples, and he still felt nauseous. He decided to take this opportunity to change the subject.

'Music? So you are a musician, like your father?' Dadafarin asked

'I'm getting there. I've been around music all my life, and I love it.' Vee replied.

Talk turned to Vee's plans for the future. He'd been playing guitar since he was eight, and could play the piano too. He joked that Boner had not wanted him to follow in his footsteps in case he proved to be more talented than him. 3's music was often accused of being formulaic, a formula that had now worked very profitably for over thirty years.

'But, joking aside, Boner actually supports me. We jam together a lot. In the basement, we've got a recording studio called The Leadroom. It's lined with lead, for soundproofing. Do you want to see it?'

'OK yes, I would like to see where you make jam.' Perhaps a bit of movement might help him recover his faculties.

Vee picked up the whisky bottle and glasses and led them through the lounge into another hallway, full of boxes, which Dadafarin hadn't been in before. A spiral staircase at one side led down into a basement. As they went down the steps, Vee told Dadafarin that he had already written a few songs, and was hoping to get a band together. There was a guy in the village who played bass whom he'd met on his last visit to the farm, and they were going to start playing together.

At the bottom of the stairs, Vee pushed open a heavy door and switched on some lights, revealing a large room with a glass partition along its full length, behind which were a drum kit, several microphones, a keyboard and a long row of guitars on stands along with an instrument that Dadafarin recognised as a sitar. One instrument, a bright orange V shaped guitar, was mounted in a case on the wall.

'I'm named after that guitar' Vee told Dadafarin. 'My dad was playing it when the band first got discovered by a record company, in a bar in London. It's a 1984 Gibson Flying Vee. He only plays it occasionally now. He's hoping Covid will be over for my eighteenth birthday, and we'll play a gig in the Red Lion together. He said he will play it again then.'

On the other side of the glass partition, Dadafarin could see two mixing desks and what appeared to be a well-stocked bar. Vee picked up a guitar, switched on an amplifier with a loud electronic thump, and fiddled with a keyboard on a stand at the side of the room. A drum track started playing as he adjusted a microphone.

'This is my latest composition, "Ain't Woke Yet" ', Vee announced through the microphone. He then started playing the guitar, and a melancholic, slightly funky beat filled the room. Initially, it reminded Dadafarin of a Bill Withers song his mother had often played, "Ain't no Sunshine", but with a hard rock feel to it. It was a catchy tune, and Dadafarin found himself tapping a foot in time with the drum machine as Vee started singing.

I ain't woke yet
But I guess there's time

There's a gender out there
That could be mine
There's a lady I know
Whose got real balls
She'll reply with violence
To any catcalls

I met a guy
Who is in fact a them
They got no truck
With no white men
Their skin is pale
Their hair is fair
But privilege sucks
When you really care

Cos I ain't woke yet
No I ain't woke yet
But I want some hate
In the name of love
I want to hate
In the name of love.

I got black friends
Some of them gay
Though I like the ladies
In a traditional way
But till I'm woke
And renounce myself
I'm just a white man
With a burden of white guilt

Vee then launched into a long and quite complicated sounding guitar solo before continuing. The tempo increased.

I've read the books
I've listened to the prophets
I've watched the videos
I've searched the closet
But I can't wake up
When I feel so alive
While the optimism I love
Stops that final dive

Cos I ain't woke yet
No I ain't woke yet
But I want some hate
In the name of love
I want to hate
In the name of love.

At the end of the song, Dadafarin clapped loudly. He was very impressed, though was not sure he'd quite understood all the lyrics. Vee switched off the amp, placed the guitar back on its stand, and switched the keyboard off. He took Dadafarin to the other side of the glass partition, and they sat on barstools as Vee poured more whisky.

'That was excellent' Dadafarin said. 'You are very talented.'

'Thank you. I'm just starting really. But I guess I got some dad privilege' Vee replied, laughing. They carried on drinking and talking for some time,

finishing half of the bottle of whisky before, at around 3am, Garriston appeared in his dressing gown.
'Lot o' fettle t'morra, lads' he said. 'Better ger um sleep.'

XXXIV
THE OPTIMISM

Life on the farm became busier as spring approached. Christmas had been a quiet affair, with just the three of them sitting around a dinner of roast duck. Having Vee staying on the farm had reduced the workload considerably. Vee seemed driven by a manic energy, and also proved to be a better cook than Dadafarin on the three nights a week he agreed to take over culinary duties. Vee and Garriston seemed to enjoy teasing each other, or 'taking the piss' as Vee called it. Dadafarin soon learnt not to be offended by jokes made at his expense, and even started 'taking the piss' out of Garriston and Vee himself. The congenial atmosphere helped the days pass quickly, and the evenings were filled with conversation and laughter. Dadafarin really enjoyed driving the tractors, and was happiest when cultivating, drilling or spraying. The farm now felt like home.

Boner visited at New Year, staying for a few days during which he reassured Dadafarin that he could stay on the farm as long as he liked. Garriston had apparently told Boner that Dadafarin was an excellent worker, and an asset to the farm. This made Dadafarin very proud, and also allayed his fears over how long he would be able to stay. They also agreed on a salary, Boner telling Garriston to back-date it to when he had first arrived. Boner left when it was announced that a new lockdown was starting on January 4th. Vee left with him, to play as a session musician on the solo studio album Boner was working on. Vee had written two of the songs that were to be on the album, one of which he had said was inspired by his friendship with Dadafarin. He promised to send Dadafarin a copy when the album was finished. Vee seemed to have healed any rift with his father over his expulsion from school, Boner admitting on New Year's Eve that he'd hated school too; he had dropped out at 16. Dadafarin missed Vee a lot after his departure, but they stayed in touch on WhatsApp. Vee was still talking about building a fire temple on the farm, and said he'd mentioned it to Boner while they were in the studio.

Apart from stopping visits to the pub, the new lockdown had little effect on life on the farm. The man who delivered their groceries acted like he was delivering toxic waste to a leper colony every time he came, parking his van a hundred metres from the house and retreating, masked, while Dadafarin unloaded their shopping from the van. Hopefully lockdown would be lifted before too long, as Noureldine was planning on visiting as soon as he could. Martin was coming with him.

Dadafarin had heard nothing from Carey since arriving on the farm, in spite of sending a few messages. Martin had met her once in London, when she had attended another demonstration. She had spent the night at his house, or rather squat as Dadafarin now realised. She had told Martin that she still liked Dadafarin, but was not yet ready to talk to him. Carey had also told Martin that Dr Venngloss was now working in a charity shop in Dorkton. The good doctor apparently seemed to have some mental health issues, as when she met up with him for a coffee, he didn't want to talk about anything except masks. Apparently, he had now decided that muzzling the public was part of a sinister strategy to keep the population under government control. Dr Venngloss had tried to persuade Carey to join him at a demonstration being held in London to oppose lockdowns, organised by Jerome Carbine's cousin Perry. It did not sound at all like the Dr Venngloss who Dadafarin knew.

Since his discussion with Vee, Dadafarin had not spent as much time following the news, except on television. Every evening after Dadafarin had cooked dinner, he and Garriston would watch the news while eating in the kitchen. The culture wars were still raging, and there had recently been protests just down the road from the farm, when a teacher had shown cartoons of the prophet Mohammed while discussing blasphemy with his class. He had received death threats, and was now in hiding. Garriston had passed an angry group of protesters outside Batley school on his way to the post office one morning. He asked Dadafarin his views on this over dinner the same even-

ing.
'Well, people should respect their religion. But not to the point where the teacher should be threatened with death and have to go into hiding. Religion causes too many problems. While I support equal rights, I have never really understood how a Muslim's right to be homophobic or transphobic is defended by people who don't like homophobes and transphobes. It was the one thing Dr Venngloss never managed to explain to me, apart from why white people can't identify as black. But I don't really think about any of it much, any more. I am too busy here on the farm.'

In fact, Dadafarin realised, he'd stopped thinking about anything much at all to do with social justice. He stayed in touch with Vee, Martin and Noureldine through WhatsApp, but apart from a recording of Vee and his father playing a new song, sent with strict orders not to show it to anyone, Dadafarin's communications with his friends were brief and irregular. He was so busy with life on the farm that he often forgot to reply to them, usually taking Shep for a walk in what little free time he had. He had now persuaded Garriston to let Shep in the house, under the proviso that Dadafarin must take full responsibility for the dog's actions. Shep now slept in Dadafarin's room, and Dadafarin had also taken over the duty of feeding him. Although his days were always busy, Dadafarin was however working his way through the many books that Boner had arranged alphabetically on long bookshelves in the lounge, reading for an hour in bed every night, and sometimes a brief spell at lunchtime. Currently, he was reading a book about bird migration, which was fascinating.

A few weeks after the demonstrations in Batley, while reading the news on his phone one morning as he ate his breakfast of porridge, Dadafarin came across a story in the Daily Post Online about some protestors gluing themselves to the gates of a refugee detention centre in southern England. He recognised the name of this detention centre; it was the same place where Ibrahim was still being held. Dadafarin suddenly realised that he'd not heard anything about Ibrahim since he'd talked with Lesley a month or so ago. Boner had recently told Garriston on a phone call that he had not heard anything about Ibrahim's case since it had been referred to the High Court. Jerome Carbine had vanished into political obscurity, and the campaign to free Ibrahim on Twitter had fizzled out months before, as the Twitter mob moved onto fresher stories. Dadafarin felt suddenly guilty that he had been distracted from Ibrahim's plight, and decided that he would call Martin and see if he had any further news.

Later, during a lull in work in late afternoon, Dadafarin climbed to the top of the haystack and called Martin. The internet had now been working for months, but climbing the haystack brought back memories of those heady days when he himself was a social justice warrior, doing his bit to make the world a better place. He missed those days when it was all still so new; the feeling of freedom, and of being a part of something great.

'Hey, Dada! How are you doing? How's farm life?' Martin greeted him.

'I am good thanks, Martin. Very busy, but I really like it here. I miss you, and I often think of our time at the party.'

'Yes, me too. But as soon as the lockdown is over, we'll be coming up to see you. Noureldine is really looking forward to it. He has a new business. I saw him last week, we've met up a few times now. He always has great weed. Have you spoken to him recently?'

'Yes, a few weeks ago. He told me he was starting a new business, but he didn't tell me what. I assumed it was something to do with cannabis.'

'Yes, him and his cousin have just started a business selling CBD oil. He wants to be well placed if they ever legalise cannabis. He wants to be a businessman.'

'He has always been a businessman' Dadafarin replied. 'Though not one on the right side of the law.' They both chuckled at this. 'I am really looking forward to seeing you both. Have you heard from Carey?' Dadafarin still thought about Carey more than he cared to admit to himself.

'Yes, I spoke with her last week. She's coming up too. Carey told me that she has forgiven you. She said that you cannot blame someone for their culture. She is really looking forward to seeing you.'

Dadafarin felt his heart start to race. 'Oh, that is wonderful news!' he exclaimed. Simultaneously, he felt excited and slightly ashamed. However, if there was one thing he had learnt since arriving in England, it was that you should accept people for what they were, and not pass judgement if it did not adversely affect you or anyone else. He was not sure he would ever be able to imagine she was a real woman, but who was he to judge? She was still a wonderful and beautiful human being. He was very glad she was coming, he realised, even if it might be awkward.

'And Ibrahim? Have you heard anything?'

'His case will be heard in a few weeks. Let's keep our fingers crossed.'

'Yes, fingers crossed.' Dadafarin crossed his fingers, remembering when he had been taught this by Boner at the dinner with the intellectual elite. 'I hope he is released in time to come up with you when you visit.'

After the call, Dadafarin stayed for a while on top of the haystack, spinning slowly around and looking across the fields. For the first time in months, he realised he felt truly happy. He had a home, fantastic friends, and had found a life which, although it was mostly hard work, he really enjoyed. He was fitter now than he'd ever been. Hopefully Ibrahim would soon be released. The government would lift the lockdown, and he would meet again all the wonderful people who had welcomed him into his new life, although he now realised he would probably never meet Dr Venngloss again. Dadafarin would show his friends around the farm and introduce them to Boner, Vee and Garriston. They would have a barbecue, and reminisce about the crazy summer of 2020. Maybe they could all live and work together on the farm, as Boner had once suggested. They would all sit around the kitchen table in the evenings as he showed them his new cooking skills, and Vee could perhaps play them some songs; they'd stay up late into the night, reminiscing and making plans for the future. Noureldine could provide cannabis for those that smoked it, and they would all drink Garriston's home-made beer. Perhaps, finally, we are at the end of all our troubles and at the beginning of happiness, Dadafarin thought to himself as he put his 'phone back in his pocket. His eyes drank in the last of what had turned out to be a spectacular sunset, perfectly matching his new mood of optimism.

As the sun dropped below the trees on the far side of the fields and the sky faded to pink, Dadafarin climbed down from the haystack and made his way towards the dairy barn. Life couldn't be better, he thought. It really was the best of all possible words. Later, he would call Carey himself. But first, there were some cows to be milked.

AFTERWORD

In mid 2020, while the United Kingdom was in full lockdown due to Covid 19, like many others I was surprised when the country suddenly and unexpectedly erupted in a series of demonstrations. The critical social justice movement had arrived on our shores, imported wholesale following the death of George Floyd at the hands of a policeman in Minneapolis. The first BLM demonstration in London surprised me for several reasons. Quite how events in Minneapolis, a city in a country with a very different history of race to the United Kingdom, was relevant in Britain was not at all obvious to me. Even more strange was the fact that the media, politicians and social influencers who had been urging us to "Stay at home, Protect the NHS, Save Lives" suddenly decided that attending mass demonstrations in the name of an American group of political activists headed by two self-professed "trained Marxists" was perfectly acceptable. The next day, I put a post on Facebook saying that it looked like the UK had been gripped by mass hysteria.

Within days of my Facebook post, my friends list

had shrunk dramatically, and I found myself being labelled a racist and a fascist by people who knew me well enough to know that I had a far more racially diverse group of family and friends than most of them. Interestingly, I was only unfriended by white, British "friends", and it appeared that the overwhelming majority of people now so aggrieved by George Floyd's death along with events that happened hundreds of years ago appeared to be white and middle-class. To say I was shocked at the sudden divisions opening up in society, supposedly in the interests of equality, would be an understatement. I decided to find out more.

Until the advent of BLM, my only interest in UK politics amounted to voting in General Elections and occasional local by-elections. Although I had spent a few years of my youth in apartheid South Africa, my only politically motivated action while there was to ignore apartheid as much as possible; I went to illegal mixed-race nightclubs, had a few black friends, and for six months I had a Sotho girlfriend, who left me after we both got arrested one night under the infamous and Orwellian Immorality Act (we were released without charge when the police realised her father was a well-known lawyer).

As I found out more about BLM, Critical Race Theory and gender ideology, I decided to start writing my thoughts down. It was while wondering how best to collate these thoughts, along with a growing collection of screenshots, articles and news stories, that I decided to write a book; I wanted to try and imagine how the social justice movement would look to an outsider. One day, an old favourite in my book collection, first read many years earlier, caught my eye. I pulled it out of the bookshelf and read it again. Within days, I had started work on this novel.

The book that inspired me was Voltaire's Candide, ou l'Optimisme. Originally published in 1759, Candide is one of the earliest satirical novels. Candide was aimed squarely at a religious philosophy endemic in France at the time, dreamt up to explain why an all-powerful God allowed such suffering in the world; this philosophy was summed up with the phrase "Everything is for the best in the best of all possible worlds". Anyone familiar with Voltaire's novella will have noticed several nods in the text of Dadafarin to Candide. The character Martin shares a name with one of the characters, and Dr Venngloss' name was inspired by Candide's mentor in Voltaire's novella, Dr Pangloss. The character of Noureldine is based on two very good friends of mine; they will know who they are, and I am sure will both forgive me. I decided not to follow Voltaire's reliance on bizarre coincidence in Candide, to make the story more believable as well as to make it flow better. My original intention was to match the 33000 words of the original, but Dadafarin ended up a fair bit longer at 55000 words.

Hundreds of hours of research over almost a year provided more material than it was possible to include in the novel. All the major events described in the book, from the BLM demonstration and the Brixton street party (which actually was held on Overton Road) to the dinner with Jerome Carbine are based on newspaper reports of real events. The processing of migrants/refugees arriving on the south coast of England is also based on current Home Office procedures. All the references to Zoroastrianism and it's history in Iran are factual; the story of the massacre which led to Ibrahim fleeing Sudan is also based on real events. I will endeavour to publish all the references on my website. Already on my website is an essay I wrote for my own amusement and to tease out a few ideas. This formed the basis of Vee's Theory of Woke.

I have read all the books mentioned in the novel and thoroughly recommend all of them, except for White Privilege by Robin DiAngelo; this dire ideological manifesto is appallingly badly written, full of opinion posing as fact, and contains "statistics" which are nothing of the sort. The Communist Manifesto by Marx and Engels is worth reading as it helps in understanding where many current leftist ideals came from.

Lastly, for anyone who thinks, as I did before starting on this project, that Vee's references to the World Economic Forum, the Great Reset and it's Young Global Leaders program, along with their drive for a cashless society tied to a social credit system, are just wild conspiracy theories, I urge you to follow Vee's advice to Dadafarin, and look at their own website.

The truth is out there, it's not in your head.

Allen Grove

Sept 2021

www.aliengrove.com

ACKNOWLEDGEMENT

I would like to thank all the people who supported me during the writing of this book. My wife J, for her unstinting enthusiasm and for providing a sounding board to bounce ideas off, and for several suggestions she made that were incorporated into the story. I would also like to thank my brother N, for his feedback, and likewise my old friend Adam. I knew both of them would give me an honest appraisal of the finished book. Thanks too to Tony Edge, who contacted me with suggestions for a few minor revisions after posting a review of the book on Amazon. His suggestions have now been incorporated into the novel.

I would also like to thank Dr Gad Saad for the permission to use his idea of victimhood poker in the game of intersectional poker played between Basil and Dadafarin in Chapter 26.

ABOUT THE AUTHOR

Allen Grove

After a youth and early adult life spent in southern Africa, Allen moved to the UK in the 1990's to pursue his career. He has lived and worked in Africa, Europe, the Middle East, India and the South Pacific, visiting over 80 countries.

Allen is the author of several articles and short stories and one previous novel. He is also a succesful photographer, undertaking commercial work as well as selling fine-art prints, under another name.

Allen currently lives in the north of England with his wife, two cats and several motorcycles.

"All men are by nature free; you have therefore an undoubted liberty to depart whenever you please, but will have many and great difficulties to encounter in passing the frontiers."

Voltaire, Candide

Printed in Great Britain
by Amazon